Bad Blood

Ann Robbins Phillips

ISBN-13: 978-1482093896
ISBN-10: 1482093898

DEDICATION

I dedicate this book to my husband, Sam. You are the encourager in my life. You are the one that makes me believe in myself, and gives me the courage to submit my stories to the readers of the world. You were right. They accepted my work with the same enthusiasm as you, and I am overjoyed. I would never have had the courage without your support and reassurance.

This is for also for other members of my family that support me. Your kind and gracious words, telling me that reaching for the stars of my dreams has inspired you to do the same, is what keeps me pressing forward with other stories. The lives of our family are weaved from the same framework set up by generations of honest, hardworking people that instilled a love for doing what is right. They taught us the basis of how to choose well when presented with decisions that could alter our lives and generations to come.

To my friends and readers that have bought my book…Thank you. You are the reason that I have any success. It would have been impossible without you telling your friends, writing reviews, and getting my book on reader groups. You have my undying love and appreciation. The books are for you and your enjoyment.

ACKNOWLEDGMENTS

I owe a great deal to a group of people that have encouraged, motivated, and supported me in the writing process. There is my sister, Violet Shults, who is by my side every page of the way-- reading, researching, and encouraging. Thank you for sticking with me. Thank you Meagan Rouse, Ginny Barnes, Wilburn Shults, and Lori Phillips. You know what you did, and I will be eternally grateful to you.

Shaen, Amy, Robin, Marty, and Holly, my children. You are my pride and joy. You made my life fun and full of joy. You chose well in companions with Angela, Eric, Emily, Lori, and Bruce (respectively). Thank you for fifteen wonderful grandchildren, some of which are already showing signs of being great storytellers!!!

Without a doubt, I have to thank Writer Groups such as Chattanooga Writers Guild, Knoxville Writers Guild, Tennessee Mountain Writers, Alabama Writers Conclave, and the North Carolina Writers' Network for the valuable tools of the trade you have put into my hands through retreats, workshops, and articles. I am not yet all

that I will be, I hope, but will continue to grow
with your sustained support.

Chapter 1
April 1888

When it was all over and done, Nathe reached down and squeezed one of his feet to see if it felt cold. It did, and his fingers loosened grains of dirt that fell onto the covers. There was no other way to explain the cold and dirt unless what he thought was a dream had really happened.

Nathe shivered and pulled the covers back over him. He wanted to go over what happened and get it clear in his mind before he woke Addie to tell her about it.

There are things that happen in life, especially in the mountains, that you can't explain, even if you want to. It is one thing to see a haint in yore dreams or think you see one in the dark of night, but it is plum scary when you see one day after day, even in sunlight. Before that summer, if anyone else had asked Nathe if ghosts or spirits were real, he would have argued to the contrary.

The dream, or whatever he could decide it was, had started with haze thicker than fog after a late spring rain in the mountains. Shapes were hard to make out. First it had been a leather boot that stepped onto a pile of wet, fallen leaves. Nathe watched as a second boot joined the other one. He looked up the body from toe to head, and knew it was me before the mist blew away and I showed my face. He had given the covers a kick and sat up straight in bed.

I aimed my long bony finger into Nathe's face and bent it back and forth urging him to follow. I walked to the door and turned back and motioned with my hand for Nathe to come on. He grabbed a coat and put it over his union suit.

When Nathe opened the door, I was halfway to the barn. All the mist had cleared. There was a faint light in the eastern sky, and the moon was at the top of the mountain and ready to slip away. There was enough light for Nathe to see that I went into the front doors of the barn.

Nathe regretted he hadn't grabbed a lantern. He could barely make out my shape as I sat on a log at the opening of an empty stable. I poked at the dried mud mixed with hay in front of me.

"Amps?"

I looked up at the dark form between me and the outside. "Open both of those doors and have a seat."

"What are you doing here?" When I didn't answer, Nathe said, "Can I hug you?"

I laughed. "Boy, we never were a bunch of huggers. Don't think that'll be necessary."

"I know, but I'm so glad to see you. It's been a long time. I didn't know who you were when you left that time in 1873. All those days of talking, and I never knew you were my grandpa. If I had only known! I never had seen a haint in my life, much less talked to one."

I laid the stick to my side. "I didn't think you would take much advice from me if you knew who I was."

"Maybe not. But I'd like to think that I was a reasonable person and would've been sensible."

"You were not a sane person back then. Yore need for revenge wiped away all reason. But you were a good person inside. I could see that from the beginning, in spite of all that you had to bear as a child."

Nathe hunkered down on his haunches. "I never thought I'd see you again…Do I call you Grandpa or Amps?"

"Amps will do just fine."

Nathe wrinkled his forehead. "You coming back makes me uneasy. Why are you here?"

I grabbed the stick again and stuck it in the mud pile. It stuck to the stick and I threw both stick and clod toward the open door. "I'm not happy about the purpose of this visit myself." I took a deep breath and blew it out between my lips. "The news I bear is not the best. I had hoped a happy life for you. No more feuding. No fighting or fussing. I'm here to warn you about something. It won't happen this year but, before long, there's going to be some things happen that will make yore heart heavy. Those happenings could even make you bitter."

"What? When will it happen?"

"It's not for me to tell you that. Not today at least. I hope to give you a second warning, but I'm not sure I'll be able to. For now, it's enough that you prepare yurself."

"How do you prepare for something that you don't know the particulars of or when it will happen?"

"For now, I can tell you that everything's not going to be rosy. I need you to remember all those lessons from when you were a young man. Things that I taught you about vengeance and hate and what it does to a man's soul. Remember, when you are hated for what you've done right, it tells you that you've been successful. Being hated for doing wrong is a different matter."

"A person can't win, can they? We're always hated by someone. Sometimes it's best to not know who yore enemies are. That way you treat them all the same."

"If I could take this all away, I'd be honored to do so. But, believe it or not, life was never meant to be easy. It's a proving ground that'll make things better in the next one. A person works on his own character and, at the same time, shapes his children like twigs. He does it by the way he responds to what happens to him. Everybody has their own trials to overcome."

The next thing he knew, Nathe was back in his bed with cold feet.

xxx

Addie turned toward Nathe. "Are you awake?"

"Yup. Have been for some time."

"Are you worried about something?"

Nathe pushed up on his elbow and faced her. "You're a light sleeper. Did you hear me get up a little while ago?"

"No. Didn't hear you get up? You were tossing and turning though. Did you dream you got up?"

Nathe laid back and crossed his arms over his forearm. "I suppose it was a dream, but my feet were plumb cold and there was dirt on my feet. I was here, and then I was out at the barn. Next thing I know I was back here. I saw Amps."

"Ahh. That 'splains a lot. What did he want? He's a rare visitor."

Nathe sat up and commenced to get ready for the day. "I'm sure glad you believe in haints. Otherwise, you'd have them come and get me and lock me away for being crazy." He grabbed his shoes, brushed off his feet, and put them on. "Why does it have to be me that he shows himself to? Why not you? You know things before they happen. You'd know what to do. But he comes to me and tells me just enough to make me live trying to figure out his riddles. He wouldn't even tell me when or what is going to happen. He thought I just needed to know now. Does he mean it will be a few months? A few years?"

Addie grabbed a housedress and slid it over the underdress she had slept in. "I've never known him to be wrong. But if you really want him to be gone, we can burn some cedar in the stove tonight and I can take some mustard and put it in a poke under yore pillow. To me, it seems best to let him talk about whatever is going to happen. It might well help us keep it from happening, whether it's next week or six years from now. You need to tell me all about it while I cook a bite to eat."

Chapter 2

May 1888

Glee winked at the other men by his side and whistled to Owen. "Come over here. I've been telling my cousins that you're one fine ladies' man. I said you could crook yore finger, and they come a-running. They have this young lady in mind that they don't believe would give you the time of day. I told them I didn't agree. We made a bet, and you need to help me win."

Owen narrowed his eyes at the men with Glee. "There ain't a woman in Jackson County that I can't get to look my way. That's a fact."

"See there boys, I told you he could do it."
Glee stomped on the foot of the skinny boy nearest
him.

He grabbed his foot and hopped. "I don't
believe it. You need to prove it, before we give
Glee or you any money."

Owen walked closer to the group. "Tell me
about this girl."

"Her name is Lottie. She's about the prettiest
little thing I've ever seen. In fact, I'd go after her
myself if I wasn't going to be married real soon."

One of the others said, "She's yore cousin!"

"Well, that too, but doubt that should make
much matter. But I'm to be a newly married man."
He winked again at the group. "Back to Lottie.
She's blossoming to be a mighty fine woman. I bet
she'd fall all over you if you come to church with
me and the boys next week. Her Papa and Mama,
Nathe and Addie Watson, bring her every time the
doors to the church are open."

"Why would you want me dating this cousin
of yorn? Why not one of these other boys?"

Glee looked around. "Well I guess there
might be one here that could get her, but I thought
my bet was better on you. They'll give a dollar if
you can court her for a month. Just lead her on a
bit, and then drop her like a cold tater. Her papa is
the one I have a bone to pick with. Him and his
family think they're better than the rest of us.
Owning land on two mountains. Lording it over all.
Lottie is pretty, but it would do him good to think a
fine man like yurself, from a well-respected family,

would not keep courting her. She'll be falling all over herself for you."

Owen figured it would be fun, if only to show the others he could. "I'll do it, but I'll only court her for one month. And I want money from each of you every time I take her out."

"Naw. One dollar total to get her to go with you, and I get fifty cents of it."

"No. I might see another pretty girl that I would rather go with and that would mess up my plans to get that one.

"I promise you will not want anyone else once you see her. Not a dollar each, but a dollar total each and every time you get her on a date. And it's 50/50."

They all shook hands.

xxx

Owen went with the other boys to church the next Sunday. It was to be a homecoming service with dinner on the ground. There would be plenty of time to meet the girls. For that was what all the young men did. They went to church to get a girl. Then they hardly darkened the doors anymore. Church was pretty much the only place Papas and Mamas let their girls go. They had a cock-eyed idea that they'd meet a good man in church and settle down. The boys laughed and talked all during dinner. After eating, there was Sunday singing that afternoon, but the younger ones sat outside on quilts and talked.

Glee pulled Owen over closer to where Lottie sat, and both squatted on the grass near the quilt. "Hey Lottie. I want you to meet a friend of mine.

This here is Owen Thompson. He's been dying to meet you."

Lottie blushed from the roots of her hair all the way down to where her neck slid into her dress. She used her hand to fan her hot face. "Good to meet ya, Owen. I've never seen you here before."

"Me and my family live in Sylva. I go to the Sylva Baptist church. But they kept telling me about the sweetest young lady named Lottie that I really needed to meet. So here I am."

The other boys laughed and poked each other.

Lottie crawled to the edge of the quilt and looked through her long eyelashes at the boys on the ground beside her and her sisters. "The church is having a taffy pull next Saturday night. You boys should come. In fact, I could use a strong young man to help at my table." She looked directly at Owen. 'Will you be there, Owen?'"

He winked at Glee and said, "I hadn't planned on it, but I might be persuaded to change my mind. That is, if I was asked nicely by a pretty young lady like you."

Lottie's sister jerked her arm and tried to pull her back from the edge of the quilt.

She jerked away. "Well, maybe I'm asking...maybe I'm not. I'll definitely be there. You come on back here, and we'll see what happens."

Owen laughed so loud that a man from inside the church came and peeked out the door.

Sugar, Lottie's younger sister, grabbed her hand and pulled her off the quilt. "I need to talk to you over by the wagon. Come with me."

"Let me alone. I'm just playing with them." Lottie looked back and smiled at Owen."

"Have you gone plum crazy? You're foolish to encourage the likes of him." Sugar jerked Lottie back around and made her look into her eyes. "He's too old for you. He's at least twenty. Papa and Mama will be mad."

"No they wouldn't. Don't you know who he is? His Papa owns the general store in Sylva. Glee told me so. They'll be glad that I turned his head. I bet they'd marry me off to him right now, if he asked."

Sugar rolled her eyes. "Then all of you are crazy. I don't like him. He's mean. And lazy. He pretends to work down at that store, but he don't do much working. Makes everybody else do his job. I've seen him when I went with Papa to Sylva."

"You're just bragging because you get to go to town with Papa. All of us have to stay home and work. Besides, you're too young to understand. I want a real man. Not a silly boy. I'm ready to be a wife."

"I'd rather be an old maid as to marry the likes of him. You'll be sorry. I may be younger than you, but you're dumber, the way I see it. You all think I'm too young to know anything, but a baby can see he is not a good person."

Sugar knew Lottie was foolishly in love and no one could reason with her.

xxx

The bet proved to be a more agreeable undertaking than Owen first thought. The men were right. She'd been easy picking. They'd been going out for three months.

Glee went to the back of the general store and found Owen laying on top of a sack of coffee in the back of a wagon of supplies for the store. "Heard you and Lottie are getting hitched."

"Yep, marrying her next week."

Owen handed him a dollar. "This is the last of the money. I let it go on too long as it is. If you think marrying her will keep the money coming in, you're wrong. That was not part of the deal. You were to drop her after a month."

"I figured as much, but she's too pretty to let any other man have her. You can have this last dollar back."

Glee reached out and took the money. "You might not want to tell her how you come to be courting her."

"Don't plan on it. It started out as a game. It was an easy bet to be won for you and me and a little extra money in our pocket. But I figured out if I wanted to keep her, I'd better marry her. There were others trying to horn in on me. I watched their faces when she prissed around and teased like she is always doing. That'll stop as soon as we're hitched. I'll keep her at home where she belongs."

The more Glee thought about it, the better he liked the idea. Lottie wouldn't know what happened to her once Owen quit trying to woo her and started making her toe the line. Oh yes. Exact pay back for the high and mighty Nathe. "Promise me you'll never tell her or nobody else about this bet."

"Don't plan on it."

Owen laid back on the coffee bean sack and thought about Lottie. Yep, she was flirty. Too flirty. He'd make sure she never teased another man like she did him. When he married her, he'd come down hard on that. She'd be his and, if any man tried to take her, his family would find his head atop a pike pole. They'd figure a Hooper did it. He laughed.

Chapter 3

October 1889

Lottie had married Owen young, at fourteen, and babies followed soon after. Some said her first was an early baby. Her Papa said honestly, "No, just a late wedding." Now, at the age of fifteen and a half, she and Owen Thompson were expecting their second child.

All her life she had heard 'You make yore bed then you have to lie in it'. This bed was about the most uncomfortable she could've imagined. Lottie had heard about mean men all her life. Then she up and married one. It made a person wonder if bad blood was more a product of the land rather than passed on within a family. She figured it out that you never really knew a man until you lived with him day in and day out, and Owen was a bad man. She stayed with him because it was what a wife did.

Owen was drunk, and today he would blow out the already flickering candle of her love. Several important things within Lottie would die. She wasn't looking for a way to leave him but, if one came along, she was not going to turn it down. But it would have to take her far away and somewhere Owen couldn't find her. Lottie honestly knew he'd kill her before he would let her go. This time in her life would burn into her memory like a hot coal on a piece of dry wood.

xxx

Lottie found her Mama sitting on the back step with a hickory limb about three feet long lying across her knees. In the other hand was a paring knife, one of three blades that Nathe had made and given to her on their first Christmas.

"Who has warts?" Lottie laughed.

"Quit yore laughing baby girl. I remember when you had seventy-two warts on yore hands. You were about fourteen and the biggest tom-boy I'd ever seen. Played with frogs down by the creek every night. You'd done it all summer long that year. You'd come in from working in the fields and head to the water. After cooling off and getting clean, you played with those ornery little toads sitting on the roots of the trees. But that year you saw a feller you liked. You'd hide yore hands behind yore back or cross yore arms and put them under yore armpits so he couldn't see them warts. If I knowed then what I know now, I'd have left them on there. But I don't rightly figure he cared about yore hands. He took one look at that purty face of yurns, and he was yorn."

Lottie swung her legs off the porch and watched her Mama cut notch after notch on the limb. "They must have more than I had. How many notches do you got to make?"

"It's that Massy gal. She came up to me after the Sunday service and pulled me to the side of the building. She stuck her hands in my face and said, 'Miss Addie, can you take these awful little things off me? My Mama says you can, but I was not to tell nobody that I came to you.' Oh my. Her poor hands were just awful. There were so many that I had to go to her house and burn a stick and use the black on it to mark them as we counted. There were two hundred twenty two on her two hands and one on each elbow."

Lottie took her toe and pushed around the pieces of wood that had fallen to the ground. "I wouldn't have done it if she talked like that about me. Pretending she didn't come to me to get the warts off. All ashamed of us."

Addie laughed loud. "I'm sure you wouldn't have. But I just let it go in one ear and out the other. She don't know no better. She's just saying what her Mama says. They all may be a hypocrites but I ain't. What I do, I do for anyone. It's a God-given gift, I think. My Mama told me how to do it, and I guess I'm telling you."

Lottie snurled her nose. "Don't tell me. I don't want none of that. People just use you. You don't get paid. Then they make fun of you."

"Lottie, girl, it's a talent. You don't take lightly those talent gifts. You use them, or one day you wake up and they's gone. I think you're more like me than any of the girls. I knew it the day you were born. Best I remember about the way I marked you was that I'd blown out fire from one of the Larkin babies that had fallen in the flames his Mama had for heating wash water. After that, I had taken off warts. Don't remember for who. Both had happened on the same day, the day I felt you move in my belly the first time. Yep, I marked you. Then when you were born with that veil over yore face..."

"Mama, stop it. I don't want to hear it. You've told me that story a hundred times. I'm not like you, not like you at all. If I was, I'd believe..." Lottie stopped and raised her eyebrows. She jumped off the porch.

"Don't be jumping off the porch like that with you in the family way. It'll make that cord wrap around the baby's neck, and it'll die in childbirth." Addie laid the stick to the side. "What was you going to say? That if you had to believe that you were like me, you'd believe what? Tell me."

"Mama, don't make me tell it. I'm NOT like you. I'm not. I don't see or know things before they happen. I can't take off warts or blow out fire. I can't stop blood. Telling something you are thinking makes it come true."

"Have you ever tried doing any of those things? You don't know till you try. I think you can. You're marked."

Lottie rolled her eyes. "Mama."

"Tell me right now what you were going to say. I mean it. I'm yore Mama, and I want to know what it's about."

Lottie sat back down on the porch and let her legs swing. Addie waited, knowing that she would tell it when she got up the nerve. Lottie lay down with her back on the porch boards and covered her face with her hands. "I still hear it. Right now I hear it. Do you?"

"Hear what? I don't hear nothing."

"You don't hear that baby crying. It's just pitiful." Lottie rolled her head from side to side. "Why don't you hear it?"

"You hear a baby crying? Oh Lottie. That ain't good."

"I know it's not good. I hear it in the early hours of the morning. I have for a week. It quits when I'm cooking but starts again as soon as Owen leaves the house. If I stay busy, the sound ain't there, but as soon as I lay my head on the pillow until I go to sleep, it cries. Anytime I am still for a minute, I can hear the cries. It sounds like a newborn baby. Tell me what it means." Lottie raised up and looked her Mama in the face. "I need to know."

"Well I'm not sure that I know what it means. But it ain't good, I figure."

Lottie stopped and cocked her head one way and then the other. Then she did it again. "It stopped. Oh, it stopped. Thank the Good Lord." She smiled and looked at her Mama.

Addie was not smiling. "I wonder why it stopped. Do you think you know?"

Lottie sucked in her breath. Big tears welled up in her eyes. "It just died, didn't it?"

"I don't rightly know, but that's probably what happened, or will happen."

"Reckon it's my baby?" Lottie laid her hands across her big, pooching stomach and then peeked up at her Mama. Addie didn't answer. They sat there, Lottie rubbing her belly and Addie watching her.

Lottie smiled big. "It just moved again, Mama. It's still alive. It ain't dead."

Addie said under her breath, "Not yet, anyway."

Lottie hugged her Mama. "Well I best be getting on home. I'll come when I can."

xxx

Owen slammed the door and watched while Addie tried to start a fire in the cook stove. There were potatoes yet to peel lying on the table and unmelted hog lard in an iron skillet on the cookstove.

"Didn't I tell you to have supper cooked and on the table when I got here?" Owen's words was slurred.

At the sound of his Papa's booming voice, Brody crawled under the rocker and peeped out over the rungs. He watched his Mama and Papa.

"We just got home. I took the children to see Mama and Papa. They hadn't seen my babies since Christmas, and I wanted to ask her to come here at the end of the month to help bring this baby into the world." Lottie rubbed her rounded belly.

Owen came face to face with Lottie but yelled as loud as if he was outside. "I told you that I want supper when I get home. That should be what you did instead of gallivanting all over the country. I work at that store to feed this family. You'd think I could expect my wife to have food ready for me when I come home."

Lottie wrinkled her nose at the smell of whiskey on his breath. "Do we have money for food, or did you drink it up on yore way home?"

Owen pushed his body against her side until he backed her away from the stove. She didn't remember how it happened but the next thing she knew her head bounced, and her bulging body, large with the baby she carried, crunched and flattened against the wall by the door. She slid down the log wall. Her fingers bled as splinters tore at the tips of her fingers. Blood ran into her mouth from the cut on her upper lip. The baby inside her gave one huge stretch, pushing against her ribs. She felt sick to her stomach. Her knees scraped against the wooden floor as she crawled out the door and to the edge of the porch. She puked on the skiff of snow that covered the ground and gagged when nothing else would come up.

Owen walked past her without speaking and got on his horse and rode away.

Lottie didn't tell a soul what had happened, and she didn't plan on anyone ever knowing.

xxx

Lottie's baby hardly moved during the next two weeks. The delivery was hard, and Addie had stayed the night as her daughter cried and wept with each need to push. About daybreak, she sent Owen to get the doctor. The wind had changed to the north, and there was spitting snow. The baby boy had come by the time the doctor arrived.

The doctor took one look at the bundle wrapped in the faded blanket and shook his head. "He's dying, Lottie."

"No, he ain't. He's asleep. He cried when he was born. He's just fine." She narrowed her eyes in anger. "His tiny face turned red, he cried, and then he fell asleep. He's been asleep ever since. He's tired from all that pushing I had to do. Mama washed him up, but he kept right on sleeping. But he's a fine little boy. About eight pounds Mama says."

"I hate it Lottie, but he's not going to live." The doctor pulled a table close to the bedside and laid him on the table and raised both fists in the air. She cringed as the fists came down, one on each side of his tiny body. The baby never flinched. The only movement was the table shook when it was jarred.

Addie ran to the door where a little head had crawled up and peeked in. She shooed Brody back and went out on the porch to be with him. She bent down and pulled his coat tighter around him. He wrapped his arms around his grandma and held on tight.

The doctor shook his head. "A normal baby would have flung his hands in the air and cried out. I tell you that he's dying."

Lottie put her hands over her ears and rocked her head back and forth on the bed. Her tears turned into a moan and then into a scream.

Lottie looked out to where Owen stood in the door and watched. His eyes locked with hers, but she was the first to look away. It would make matters worse for her to yell at him for the part he played in this baby's death, what with her Mama and the doctor there. If she let them know what he'd done, there'd be hell to pay when they left.

"Make funeral plans today. He'll be gone by morning. The snow will have melted and the ground might still be soft enough to dig a grave if they do it tomorrow. Won't be easy but it can be done." The doctor took the baby from the table and laid him in Lottie's arms.

Lottie swaddled him in the faded blanket and the baby quilt she'd finished the week before and tucked him near her body. She turned her face to the wall and crumpled her face. She tasted blood as she bit her lips to squelch the scream. *I wish Owen was the one dead.*

Owen opened the door wide and motioned to the doctor to leave. "Thank you. We'll take it from here. Don't think we need you anymore now."

The doctor looked at Lottie's back and then at Owen. "I can give Lottie something to help her sleep."

Lottie turned back to the doctor with tears in her eyes.

"Nawh. She'll be fine. It's not like it's the first baby that ever died. We have another living one to take care of. That'll keep her mind off *this'n.*"

Lottie's took her lower lip between her teeth and bit harder. Her body shuddered from the pain, and she tasted blood. Tears ran down the side of her nose and into her mouth.

"I hardly think that would make her feel any better about losing this one." The doctor raised his eyebrows at Owen.

"Well, don't matter much how we feel, now does it. We have to get up and go on about our lives. Can't lay in bed and wallow in our troubles. The rest of us will need supper tonight and breakfast in the morning. That don't change. Her jobs will keep her busy and take her mind off of it."

The doctor looked at Lottie and shook his head. "Are you going to be all right?"

She nodded but stared at the wood cookstove in the corner, stared even as tears ran down her face. Talking was too hard. If she spoke out loud to the doctor or anyone else, she knew she might tell them what a horrible excuse for a man she had married. They had probably already guessed it.

xxx

Her baby lay beside her all night. Lottie never slept a wink.

"My little, sweet baby boy, Jacin." She whispered as she pulled his tiny body across hers when she turned over to face the door. She laid him in the crook of her right arm. She planted little kisses on his head and listened to tiny breaths of air as he breathed in and out.

It was about four in the morning when the breathing stopped. Lottie didn't call out to anyone.

Her Mama had gone home to take care of her Papa
and taken Brody with her. She needed a few
minutes more of peace with this baby that would
never suckle her breasts. A baby that she would
never cradle in her arms again after today. She
knew it was no use going any further with that kind
of thinking.

*What makes a man think that if you have
another child that the death of a newborn would
not be felt just as deeply? It couldn't have been
worse had it been my only one. I'd lived with it
inside my belly for the eight months that I knew
that I was in the family way. I sang to it, talked to
it, and thought about names-even thought about its
future.*

Future. She'd daydreamed that this baby
might be the one that would grow up and take her
away from this prison. This boy or girl might get a
good education and find work in some big town.
Some kind of work that didn't make a person's
hands bleed from briers after working in the field
or their skin tough like tanned leather from the sun
beating down on their back. It would decide that
his mama should live near him and come and get
her. But all her dreams had died right along with
this sweet baby boy. Jacin Nathaniel Thompson.

That was the day she stopped dreaming.
Stopped hoping. This life was her own doing, and
there was no need for anyone else to know how
foolish she'd been. It was the time she made up
her mind that, come what may, she'd made this
bed, and it looked like she was going to have to lay

in it. That was unless someone could get her out of
here alive and not in a wooden box.

Chapter 4

April 1898

Nathe Watson purposed to stop by my abandoned cabin. Last night he had dreamed a strange dream, and he knew it was time for another meeting. He had a gut feeling that today he would get to see my face like in 1873 and, for a brief time, in 1888. I had died several years before Nathe was born. I remember well when he came back to North Carolina from over the mountains of Tennessee. He was full of hate and ready for revenge. We had talked like old friends. It was hard not to tell him how we were kin. He was a fine young man, but the troubles he had lived with would have made most any person have hate in his heart. I didn't want it to stay there and ruin his life, because that is exactly what can happen if you give a home to hard feelings. In 1888, I gave a brief warning of coming trouble. The trouble he was about to face in the next few weeks.

xxx

The eastern sky was dark with no hint of sunrise. Overhead, there were an untold number of stars. There was a soft glow through the tops of the trees from the new moon. It would be a good hour before it would set beyond the mountain. Nathe Watson trimmed the wick of his lantern. He took a broomstraw, stuck it to a coal of fire in the kitchen stove, and touched the oil-soaked material. Light flashed, and he lowered the glass cover over the flame. Then, he rode his horse by the flickering light of the oil lantern to Rich Mountain. The moon that had cast its strange glow during the trip slid behind the shadows of the trees in front of him. The darkness was thick without the moon's light. He was thankful that the lay of the land was as clear in his mind as if it was lighted. He was familiar with every risky place he would need to put down a steady foot.

By the time he passed the road that led to the house where he and Addie had set up housekeeping twenty years ago, the early red sparks of light lit much of the eastern sky. When they left this house and moved to Double Top Mountain several years ago, they had given the small farm to Davie Tom, Addie's son from her marriage to a soldier killed during the Civil War.

Nathe blew out the lantern. The eastern sky now showed a greyish yellow light that outlined

the mountains to the east. Not long after, it took on
a bright red glow that made the mountain look like
it was on fire. He rested and watched until the sun
peaked above the trees and shot streaks of light
upward into clouds lined with red and gold. It was
a sight that warmed the soul and made it glad to be
alive. There was nothing to compare to watching a
sunrise and the colors that it cast. For Nathe, a
sunrise meant new beginnings and gave hope that
things today might, somehow, be better than
yesterday. A new day. God's way to give man a
new start. Although he maintained a hopeful
attitude in his philosophy about life, today he
feared there might not be many more sunrises for
him. It sure had passed fast. Life had rushed by
like blowing out a deep breath. He couldn't help
but wonder if he had done all that he should have
done for his family. But when you are face to face
with the end, it's harder to set right any wrongs
you've done or make plans to change the path of
yore life. You have to live with the results of the
life you made. He planned to use these last days of
his life to get a clear look at his family and tie up
any loose ends.

      Nathe stopped on the hill above my home
place and slid off the horse's back to the ground.
He stretched his tired, aching body and walked to
the edge of the path. He grabbed the tree to steady
his tired, wobbly legs and looked down. The roof
of the house was completely caved in. The walls
were gone, rotting and going back to dirt, all except
for the logs of the back wall that was held up by
two large trees. A few saplings grew from tree

roots on each side of the wall and scotched it up. Nathe's heart quivered in his chest at what looked like a shadow of a man standing by one of the trees at the corner of the house. Just as quickly as it was there, it was gone. This place was where he had first met me. He had eaten by a fire that I had kindled and tended for days on end. This was the place he ran to when things didn't make sense anymore. He came to the man that he felt had more wisdom than anyone he knew. This was where he was taught how dangerous the feelings for revenge are, and where those thoughts could lead you. At least I had tried to teach him. Every day was a new test.

Beside the road, my barn still stood…its logs weathered and dark from years of changing weather. The whole structure leaned, the roof rotted away. The fact that it still stood was odd…a reminder of my family and the lives that had been gone for years. But this was a scrap of our life left to testify that we had been here. But soon it would all be gone. When all the planks rotted away and turned back to dust, like the people that lived here, all of the signs of our presence would disappear.

If Nathe was going to see me again, he knew it would be on Rich Mountain. The place I loved till my dying day. In the darkness of the night, as I had stood by his bed, he had read my lips as I formed the words "Thunderhead Point". There was a reason it had to be at that very place. It was another mile up the winding road and on the side of the mountain. He mounted his horse and weaved back and forth on the road that had been made generations ago by our family.

XXX

The remainder of the climb was slow for him.
Nathe stopped and took a coughing spell. He
struggled to catch his breath.

The higher on the mountain he rode, the more
the mist and fog settled into the limbs of the tree.
The path became visible only a few feet in front of
him at any given time. Water flowed from springs
down gullies and deep trenches and onto the path.
The horse's hooves slid on large, flat rocks.

An hour later, Nathe had ridden three-quarters
of a mile due to the roughness of the road. But
now the foggy cloud was below him, and the mist
had settled to give way to blue skies and warm
sunlight overhead. The heat would have dried the
fog and mist below by the time he came back this
way.

He'd made no plans to go to the house farther
up the mountain, the place where the Hoopers had
killed the biggest part of the Watson family in a
massacre over thirty-five years ago. Even though it
had been a long time, he could close his eyes and
feel like the child he had been then. A lad of nine
years old. He could still close his eyes and see the
heads on pike poles outside his house, feel the
goose bumps on his legs and arms, and hear the
whimpers coming from his mouth without knowing
it was him that cried. No, he didn't want to go
there now. Glee, Addie's nephew, the son of her
brother Marshall, lived in the house and had for a
couple of years. He was their share-cropper. At
least he was supposed to be. Glee didn't seem to

work very much and was not much of a go-getter for a young man. Not like Nathe and Addie's children. But some people seem to be happy with less in the way of worldly goods, and there's nothing wrong with that he supposed, if they pay their bills and are fully satisfied relying on the mercy of others for most of the necessities .

At Thunderhead Point, Nathe got off the horse. He stooped down atop a rock that jutted out over the valley. He stared at the land that stretched outward for miles in all directions. One mountain faded into another, stacked like cord wood plum near to Virginia, he guessed. He looked down the side of Rich Mountain. The only thing different today than when he lived here years ago was that there were more houses scattered through the woods, each marked by chimney smoke that rose from fires that cooked their breakfast.

Nathe spoke aloud. "What am I supposed to do? Do I really think Amps will meet me here? Even if he does, what's it about?"

He didn't expect an answer. What he needed was to feel my presence, to hear my voice. I had been a man that had killed for revenge. But I realized, in death, that fighting was not the best way to settle quarrels. There's not a man that wouldn't give their eye teeth to talk to someone that had died and ask questions. Nathe believed the nearest you could come to truth and wisdom was from a dying man. I told him of my repentance. I had shared some things that were a dead's man's regrets.

What Nathe really wanted was for somebody to tell him about what it was like to die. What would happen? What should he do to prepare his

family for his death? Nobody wants to think about
dying until they have to. He figured there was
nobody that could tell him what it was like unless it
was me. I'd know. The dream a few years ago had
warned him of hard times in the family would
come, but I had not told him by the time it
happened he would be sick and almost to the point
of death.

My few words last night made Nathe think I
wanted to talk about some kind of danger. Those
words that I had said to Nathe had been, "Revenge
is like the trap of Jeffries' Hell. They's going in
there if you don't stop them. If they go in, they
can't get out. The trees on Rich Mountain hold
dark secrets." I'd whispered Thunderhead Point,
and then was gone into the darkness of Nathe's
bedroom.

Jeffries' Hell. Nathe had awakened and
pondered this like I knew he would. All western
North Carolina and Eastern Tennessee knew about
Jeffries' Hell. It was only one of the many hells
that were scattered through the mountains. There
were two on Rich Mountain. A 'hell' is a thicketty
place of tangled laurel and small spruce pines
scattered along the banks of mountain streams.
There's grief to any man who crawls too deeply
into the branches. Once inside, it's almost
impossible to turn around or make yore way to the
outside. Limbs slap you in the face and branches
and rough bark tear yore clothes. It surrounds you
like a coat that's too small, and it's possible to
spend days there without food or water before you
can escape. Hours feel like days, and days could

feel like months. Some never made it out alive.
Their bones found years later when someone
cleared a section of the creek bank to make way for
watering their animals or carrying water. Jeffries'
Hell is one of the biggest. It is two miles square
and at the head of Tellico Creek in the rainbow
country of North Carolina.

Yep, revenge is hell. Hoopers and Watsons
had fought bloody wars to avenge murders and
other real and supposed wrongs for several
generations. Would there be enough time to bring
his family through the hell…to pry away the
fingers that picked and clutched at them? That
threatened to stop their escape and destroy each
one? Nathe could only hope and pray.

Chapter 5

"I thought you might visit here today." My
voice sounded like a hand rubbing over gravel,
scratchy and rough.

Nathe turned toward the voice. "You said
Thunderhead Point, and so here I am."

I leaned against a tree. Nathe looked at my
same too-large shirt and breeches that I had worn
years ago. My appearance showed no aging. Nathe
felt like he was staring into Addie's looking glass.
Time and age had caused him to take a lot of
appearances akin to me. We both had high cheek
bones and leathery skin, eyes drooped with a fold
of skin on the outside of our eyes. Family traits
from the family that came to this land in search of
freedoms.

I laid a hand on each elbow as I crossed my arms. My skin was dark with white blotchy patches on my hands.

Nathe looked at his own hands and back at mine. He looked at the lump at the base of my little finger. Almost like another finger. Nathe didn't have one of those.

"Sit down sonny boy, and I'll *jine* you." I reached out and pointed to a large rock near the tree.

Neither of us spoke for several minutes, deep in our own thoughts. I thought on the families that come after us. Generations to us. Many that I would never know. Nathe worried about the family he had now.

Nathe said, "You know Amps, I left this mountain to try to leave behind all that's happened here. I moved to Mills Ridge. I wanted to be free to work my land without politics, schemes, or any reason to think about revenge. Too much happened on Rich Mountain, things I want to be past and forgotten. I'd hoped to work hard with my hands, raise my family, and make a living 'till I died. I'd *druthe*r take a beating as to get in this feuding mess again."

"I considered moving away at one time myself, but it was when I was a child and planned to run away. Mama offered to help me pack. I started crying and never wished to leave again. I fought for what was mine after that. Any hint that someone was goin' to take what was mine was enough to set me off. Things don't matter anymore. People do."

"It appears that I'm a dying man." Nathe cupped his chin and mouth in his hand. He squeezed his eyes shut. He opened them and looked at me. "As I watched the sun rise this morning, it made me realize a few of my simple pickings. Things that I'll miss. I know *fer* a fact that I had druther behold a sunrise as see a sunset. I'd druther look down into the valley as look up toward the mountain. And, for the most part, I *enjoys* seeing a body a'coming toward me than one a'going, especially if they're my children. My trip here today found me fixed on things that I feel meaningful in life. You're right though. People are the most meaningful in the end."

I nodded and let Nathe talk. "If you feel you're near death, you want to grab the things of life with both fists. You try to get them into *yore* hands and hold on tight. Especially those you love. I think I'll go out of this life kicking and screaming."

Nathe stood and looked up toward the top of the mountain. "Mama once told me that she talked Papa into moving to the top of Rich Mountain so as to see the day a'coming *and* a'going. She'd grab a view of the sunrise with both eyes as she worked, she told me. Many an evening I've watched her stand and view the sun set over that mountain." Nathe pointed toward the western mountains where clouds settled over the top. "Sometimes she had tears in her eyes. I didn't know why. I was just a boy. Life was easy for me. But with all the killing that went on in our family, I now figure she was worried about dying and leaving that view. I guess she could have been worried about leaving us."

Nathe took a deep breath and continued. "Sunsets are pretty but I say give me the east side of the mountain any day of the week. Sunrises are what I love the most. That's why I traded the barrel of a hog rifle for land on the east side of Double Top Mountain and moved my family there. One hundred acres running the entire length of Mills Ridge. But I also traded it to get more land to leave my children. Something that would always remind them of me."

I folded my hands together and rolled my thumbs one over the other in a twiddle. "Anywhere in these mountains a man can live is like heaven on earth. It's a hard place to leave…even in death. And if you have to leave, it draws you back. YOU drew me back." I squeezed my eyes shut and turned my face away.

Nathe had tears in his eyes. "I know I've been rambling something silly like. Things that don't make sense to nobody but me. I jump from one memory to another. From one thing that I think I'll miss when I die to another thing. Why does life have to rush by? Why can't it be slow? Death is a thief. It steals everything good. It seems to allow the mean person to live longer than the good. It wants to pull you out when you're just beginning to reap yore rewards for raising a good family."

Nathe sat down and leaned his head against the tree. "Children are a blessing, but they weigh heavily on yore heart clear to yore dying day. We raised Addie's son, Davie Tom, and have two more sons, Cling, and Asa. There are four daughters, Mariah Grace, Maggie Lucinda, Lottie, and Sadie Ruth that we call Sugar." Nathe grinned at me.

"Do you remember telling me how many children I'd have?"

I nodded. "They're mighty fine children, son."

"Well you were right, down to the very last one of them. Addie and I talk about that a lot. The more children a family has, the greater the joy. But I know it makes a more likely chance that someone is going to be a bad seed. There is bad blood on both the Watson and Hooper sides. Thank God Davie Tom is settled and seems to be doing all right over here on Rich Mountain. You've not visited while I raised these children. You seem only to come when something is going to happen. Is something bad going to happen? Am I to start looking for trouble before it finds us?"

I walked to the edge of the mountain, puckered up my lips, and spit to the side. "Bad blood. I've studied on that thought for some time. That's what people have said about us for a long time. They say, 'Them Hoopers and Watsons have bad blood.' I reckon there might be something to it, but I'm more apt to believe that how a person turns out is more to their raising. Bad examples are more powerful than bad blood to drive a man in the wrong direction."

Nathe frowned. "Why does something have to happen right here at the end of my life? I've lived a good life. Tried to do what was right. I'm too old and tired for this. I've struggled all my life, worrying about the Hoopers and the Watsons staying on the straight and narrow and away from this feud that's plagued our family for generations. I wanted to prove the talk about our past is not the way we are now. Who will do it when I am gone? We still live in these mountains, and I guess we always will."

I coughed from deep in my chest, then cleared my throat and spit. My voice was stronger. "Hard feelings were nursed by our two families with stories of quarrels and generations of hatred and revenge. I'm as guilty as the next *feller*. I threw logs on the fire lots of times with talk to my sons of hatred toward the Hoopers. If there was bad blood, I was much of the reason. But there's not a person alive or dead that could truthfully say that you haven't tried yore dead-level best."

Both men stared at the layers of mountains. I spit on the ground between my legs. I looked at Nathe. "I don't know when you'll die, if that's what you want to know. It's a mystery known only to the one that created you. In fact, I know very little about anything exceptin' I'm here to warn you. It's time to end these hard feelings once and for all, son. If not, there's not going to be anyone left. Our family name will be just a memory. The Hooper name will be too. We'll just be a story some papa tells to his children whilst they sit around the fire at night."

Nathe walked over and stood with me at the edge of the mountain. "It don't make sense to me. Yore talk is a riddle. But I do know, more than most, what pure meanness and hatred can do to a person. How it can make you want to kill. Tell me who is stirring up the feud again. I want to know."

"I can't tell you." I kicked at a pile of rocks, and they rolled down the mountain with the sounds echoing back as they hit from one rock to another. "It's like the rocks falling off the mountain or my whistling to the wind. One small sound echoes over and over. If two whistle or kick at rocks, it makes the sound louder and last longer. There is a sound of trouble in the air. This one talks to that one. Plans are made to hurt another. People do it all the time. But with our families, it usually ends with somebody dying. Always has."

"I can't stop someone if I don't know who it is. I can't warn them. You have to tell me. Tell me what's going to happen so I can stop it." Nathe rushed his words and then struggled to get his breath. He bent over and tried to cough up the wad in his throat. He was a very sick man.

"I told you I am not sure who all is a part of this plan. But I do know you'll be back to this very place on Rich Mountain sometime this year. This spot will be where it ends. It seems that you and me will have to decide if what starts this is worth a man being killed. My hope is that it will not come to that decision. I want it to end on its own, without bloodshed."

"What will end?" Nathe yelled. His voice sounded scratchy, and he started the hacking cough again. When Nathe rose from his fit of coughing, I was gone.

Chapter 6

Walking down the mountain was easier than climbing, and the cough slacked up. At the forks of the road by my home, instead of going toward Mills Ridge, Nathe turned and went to Davie's house.

Davie was at work in the field by the old hog pen. Nathe walked around the pond that stood full of water from the spring rains, and went to where Davie was kicking dirt to cover the seeds as they fell from his hands into the rows.

"Whatcha planting, son?"

"Papa. What are you doing on this mountain? Is Mama faring well?"

"*Yore* Mama is fine. I just come to check on things around here. What kinda seeds you got there?"

"Sugar beets. I wanted to do sugar cane, but Pearline's family raised sugar beets, and that's what she likes. So that's what I'm planting."

"Smart boy. It pays to keep the cook happy." They both laughed.

"Tell Mama that Pearline is in the family way. The baby should be here sometime in October."

Nathe slapped Davie on the back. "That's just wonderful, son. You'll make a fine Papa. You were so good to yore brothers and sisters as they each came along. That baby will have a good family."

"Thanks, Papa. We didn't think we'd get to have any babies. Pearline had some injuries as a child and the doctor said she couldn't get in the family way. This was a mighty fine surprise. I hope Mama can come when it's time for the birth. Pearline's family moved to Tennessee and won't be able to be back here, I don't reckon."

"You couldn't keep *yore* Mama away, I don't think. She'll be so proud for you." Nathe loved the way that Davie's face shone with pride. "Can you take a minute? Let's sit under a shade tree for a little talk."

"Sure. What's wrong?"

"I didn't want you hearing this from anybody else, so I thought I'd come by and tell you myself. The doctor said I have some kind of heart condition, and he didn't think I'd live long." They sat down on the ground but, at that news, Davie jumped back up. "No, Papa. Are they sure?"

Nathe leaned against the tree, glad for the shade and a little rest. "He said, once in a rare while, a person might live longer than a few months, but he didn't know if I would or not. I hope to live a while, of course. Got a few things that I feel need my attention before I meet my maker."

"I'll just pray that you live a long time. Is there some place up in Asheville you can go to the doctor? Or maybe up in the New England States? I could go with you to see. We could take a train."

"I figure we all got a certain number of days to live and when mine is up, it's up. I just hope the good Lord lets me live to take care of pressing business."

"Is there anything I can do? Do you need me to help put in yore crop this year?

"Cling lives closer than you, and he can help. Asa left last Saturday for Asheville. A friend of his got them jobs building railroad trestles over rivers and creeks. Mariah and her husband Beauregard Hoyle, Maggie, and Sugar can help, too. We don't see much of Lottie since she married Owen. Don't know why they don't come more often. We're not that far away."

Nathe frowned. "I've heard things about Owen and Lottie. They say he takes to drinking on occasion. Not sure that he's hurt her, but they say he gets real mean when he gets to drinking the 'shine. Can't hold his liquor at all."

"Well I better never hear that he's hurt her." In the back of his mind, he remembered what I had said about teaching his children to feud. "I'd get the law after him for sure."

Davie drew his forehead into furrows that looked as deep as the rows he'd made in the field. "The law don't get involved much in family matters. What a man does in his home is purty much his own business. You know we have to take care of things like this ourselves. I'd be more than willing to stop this right now."

It was times like this that Nathe could feel the risings of anger from deep within him. If someone hurt his family, he could hurt them. He knew that. A person has to walk a fine line between defending his family and being downright angry enough to destroy another person. There were a few people that could make him that angry.

"Do you see much of Glee?" Nathe asked.

Davie rubbed the back of his neck. "I see him sometimes. He comes off this way if he's going to Sylva. I went out last week and made him stop and talk to me. I asked him what crops he's growing, and he got real angry and told me it was none of my business. The ground up there is pretty poor, I reckon. But he didn't make mention of that. It's not rich like it used to be the last few times that I tended it. It's like it don't have nothing more to give. Crops don't want to grow good and about all it can do is to produce weeds. Everyone around here says crops have not done good anywhere in Jackson County for a few years, and they's getting worse all the time. I'm not sure what we'll do once it don't grow enough vegetables for food on our table. It may come to that. A person may have to move away to feed his family. "

Nathe didn't want to think his children could move away from him and him not be able to see them. "The last two years Glee has lived there have been slim years, if what he gives us in share

cropping is anything to measure it by. He came by
two weeks ago and asked what I'd take as *pay*
instead of crops shared. He said his family needed
the food. I asked where he'd get the money but he
hem-hawed around. I figured his Papa might give
him the money. So I gave him a fair price that I
could accept. I could have told him not to worry
about paying this year, but felt he needs to learn the
hard lessons of making ends meet for a family.
Have you heard anything about how he might be
going to get the money?"

Davie picked up a stick and threw it into the
woods behind them. "Not a thing. He tries to stay
away from me. We were friends as children. We
played together when we all visited Grandpa
Clay's house, but it's like he don't want to have
nothing to do with me now."

Nathe struggled to get to his feet. Davie
reached out and steadied him. "Something else is
wrong. I can feel it."

"I've seen Amps again."

Davie said, "Is it a sign that you're going to
die real soon? Did he come to guide you over?"

"I think it's more than that. I talked with him
on the mountain earlier today. He's telling me that
the feud is brewing again. Something is going to
happen. I fear there'll be death."

"Can I do anything?"

Nathe placed his right hand in Davie's right
hand and, with his left one, he grabbed Davie's
upper arm. He started a handshake but instead
pulled him close and hugged him. "I don't even
know what I can do." He loosed Davie and said, "I
best be getting back. It'll be dark before I can get
there. *Yore* Mama will be worried if I'm too late."

XXX

Nathe went to the mill in Balsam to get a promise that they would buy any extra corn he had this year like they had the last. That money would help them buy the staples for the winter like sugar, coffee, and such like. He hoped to be able to stay strong enough through the growing season to bring it to harvest, even if he had to hire someone to help.

It was hard to find hands to work on a farm. More and more of the children of families in the mountains were leaving as soon as they were old enough. They set off for Asheville or even further north in search of jobs and a better life. It was sad, really. Mama's and Papa's depended on letters from them just to know they were alive. Some would die without seeing any of their family again.

Nathe sure hoped his children stayed close by. Addie would be in need of them when his time came to pass. She'd need her family around her. He really needed them to help him now but doubted he could count on them. Cling was married and had his own farm to work. So did Davie. Mariah's husband had moved her out a ways, near enough for visits but not close enough to help with crops and work on the farm and still be able to farm their own land. He didn't want to think about depending on Owen, Lottie's husband. He was as useless as tits on a boar hog. The only thing he seemed good at was keeping Lottie in the family way, giving her more and more children to tend to. Not that Lottie minded. She loved her children. But if it wasn't for her papa's help, and Nathe supposed some from Owen's uppity family, they'd starve.

Nathe needed a good crop this year. But with everybody so busy, he needed to find a farm hand to help, even though they were hard to come by.

With the assurance they'd gladly take any extra corn he could spare, Nathe left the mill feeling better about the future of his family.

xxx

"Mister, did I hear you tell the mill owner that you needed a farm hand?"

Nathe looked the man from head to toe. He looked strong and eager. And a little familiar. "I did say that. Are you looking for work?"

"Yes I am. I came over from Tennessee. I've been logging and working on a road over the mountains for the past two years. I thought I might be able to get work on the railroad in this area, but they're using prisoners to lay the rails. I guess if a man got hungry enough, he might be willing to commit a crime in order to get those jobs. At least they feed and house you."

"I don't think that'll be necessary." Nathe smiled. "You say you're from Tennessee. What part?"

"Upper east Tennesse. Cocke County."

"Well, I'll be. I lived in Cocke County for ten years of my life from age nine to nineteen. What's yore family name?"

"Radford. I'm Beckley Radford. You can call me Beck. My Papa was Riley Radford."

Nathe laughed hard and slapped Beckley on the back. "You were a little feller when I left. Not much bigger than a jackrabbit. I know yore Papa well. I lived with my cousin, Jemena Milsaps. She owned a farm over a ways from yore Papa. "

"I remember yore family. I knew Jemena after she married a man by the name of Webster. But I heard she was married to a Milsaps before him."

"Well any Radford from Cocke County Tennessee is welcome to work for me. Radfords are hardworking and honest people. Yore Papa was the most kind-hearted man I ever knew. He taught me to hunt. Jemena's first husband died in the war while I was a lad, and it was yore Papa that taught me things a man should know. Hunting and fishing. How to clear fields and plant crops. He let us borrow tools. There wasn't anything he wouldn't have done to help us. A mighty fine neighbor. This might be a chance to repay some of his kindness. Is yore Papa still living?"

"No. Him and my mama both passed away three years ago with the fever. That's why I needed to get away from there. I was the child that lived nearest to them. It fell on me to take care of them through their sickness. But I'm glad to say I was able to do that. The memories were too hard after that. I may go back someday but, for now, I'll be around here. I came to Jackson County on business but decided to stay a spell."

They talked about pay. There would be money a little along so he could pay room and board where he was living, but the final payment came at the end of the season. It was sealed with a

handshake and a promise from Beck to be at
Nathe's place at daybreak the next day.

Chapter 7

"Sugar, hold still and let me finish. If not, you could bleed to death." Addie held the wiggling Sugar snug against her chest and wrapped a rag over the cut. "And when I passed by over thee and saw thee polluted in thine own blood, I said unto thee, Live, Sadie Ruth Watson, live....And when...."

"Mama, ain't our names Millsaps? Why do you use Watson when you are stopping blood? One day you tell us to use Millsaps, and now today you are using Watson again."

"Well it only works if you use the real name. The whole name. Do I need to tell you that story all over again? Papa says Millsaps some of the time because he lived with that family in Tennessee as a child, but he's a Watson and uses that most of the time. So you's a Watson by blood, and I need to use that. My family still refuses to call me a Watson. Ha! Like a name makes any difference."

Sugar pushed her lips together to hide the grin that wanted to spread clear across her face.

"You little fox. You know all this, but you just like to hear me tell it."

"Well, yes I do, but I also want you to stop pushing yore fist against that cut on my arm. It ain't that bad. It has bled a lot, but I don't think it's deep. I cut it on a wire when I crossed the fence down by the chicken house."

"What was you doing crossing that fence?" Addie bent her head to the side and narrowed her eyes. "Tell me you didn't go and meet that Chastain man. You cut across the field and through the woods, didn't you?"

"All right then, I won't tell you, if you don't' want me to." Sugar jumped up and ran to the water bucket. She grabbed a dipper full and went to the back door.

"You meet him again, and I'll take a switch to you, even if you are almost grown. You have no business meeting him like that. He's near to thirty, if he's a day. He's too old for you. That Chastain family don't even like you, and you know it. What a man that age wants with a girl yore age is not a pretty thing. You listen to me. He's a womanizer. I hear tell he is with all kinds of women. I already have one daughter that made a bad choice in her man."

"It's not like Tolliver or me care what they like. It's our lives. And he says he loves me. I know I love him. He even said we would get married someday. It can't be soon enough for me. When I seen him, I just knew I loved him."

"I think I need to lock you in the barn. What has got into you? Don't you go near him again."

"Age ain't important. You're older than Papa. You told me so yurself. He was probably too young for you. But you loved him, and you got married. I had to go and see Toliver today. He's going to Asheville for a month to visit family, and I'll miss him. So I got up early, found a four leaf clover and put it in my shoe, and went to meet him."

Addie pointed her finger at Sugar. "Don't get marrying in yore mind. You was hoping he would be the first one you met so he would be the one you married.   I hope you met somebody else on the way to meet him. What is it about spring that makes young girls crazy as they can be? Looking for four leaf clovers to find love. Ha! Makes me wish it was winter again."

Sugar started pouring water over the cut before she got from the door to the edge of the porch. "Hello Lottie," she called back to her sister that had rushed up on the porch and disappeared into the kitchen.

"Don't put water on that cut. I just got the blood stopped. You'll make it bleed again." Addie turned away from the door and watched Lottie sit down on the bench at the back of the table.

"I slipped out and came over when I heard Papa was sick. Somebody said that the doctor came and left shaking his head. Then I heard he was dying." Lottie appeared out of breath, like she'd

been running. "Is he going to get better? Nothing
bad is going to happen to him, is it Mama?"

Addie sat across from her daughter and stared
at the tears running down her left cheek. "Child
we've not seen you in a month. Where have you
been?"

Lottie pulled her hair tighter against the right
side of her face and looked down. "I'm sorry
Mama. I've been so busy. Owen thinks I
shouldn't be coming over so much. He says we
need to make our own home and family. I'm
supposed to leave you all and stay at our house and
do what he says, just like the good book says."

"I'm not asking you to come over all the time,
but maybe you can come at least once a month.
Where are them babies? I know that good for
nothing Owen don't have 'em. He ain't going to
tend to a baby. Naw, of course not."

"Don't talk about my husband like that. I love
him. He says it's not good for me to be walking
two miles while I'm in the family way. He would
be mad as a hornet if he knew I run all the way
here today."

"Well he's right about that. And, child, don't
you be running. You'll shake that baby out. Or
flop it around so that the cord will wrap around its
neck. Do you hear me? I do want you to take care
of yurself, but Owen should bring you over in the
wagon. We ain't seen him in six months. What's
he got against us anyways?"

"Let's not fight Mama. I want to know about
Papa. That's what I came for. Is he going to die?"

Addie walked to the back door and threw out a
pan of dishwater. "The doctor says he thinks it's
his heart. Sounds like it's giving out, he said. Said

it could be a few months to a few years. He told us
that there have been two or three that he knew of
that lived several years, but more often they just
die in their sleep or while they're working. I don't
know if it's true or not that he's going to die, but
Papa took it as the gospel. He only heard the *few*
months part. He just shut up his ears after that. He
left on his horse this morning. He said that dying
looked like it was going to be too quick. That he
had too many things to do. That his family needed
him."

"We do need him. I need him. I don't want
him to die." Lottie put her head down on her arms
and twisted her head back and forth. "Mama, if
Papa dies, I want to die too."

Addie jerked Lottie's arms and made her look
her in the face. "I don't want to hear those words
out of yore mouth again. Do you hear me? Yore
Papa may or may not die, but you're stronger than
you think. Ain't no Watson, or Hooper for that
matter, that would talk any such way."

Lottie pulled a lock of her hair across her
cheek. When her Mama leaned to the side to see
what she was trying to cover up, she grabbed
another hand full of hair and tried to hide more of
the right side of her face.

"Get yore hand down, child. Let me look at
that."

"It ain't nothing. I was holding August in my
lap, and she jerked and fell backwards against my
face."

"I don't believe you. That sorry thing Owen
hit you, didn't he?"

"Mama."

"I never have felt good about yore union with that man, and I can't believe you didn't feel it too. You were born with a veil over yore face. Inside you is the gift. You're able to see things. See them as they are and not just the way they seem. I was born with one, and my Mama was born with one. Our family is given second sight. We know things before they happen. Granny Hooper was there when you was born. She said, 'Lordy, daughter, we have a sighted girl. She will see and know things. Like her Mama and her Granny Hooper, she is. She knew you had gifts."

Lottie turned her legs around to the end of the bench, bent at the waist, and laid her upper body on her legs and her arms around her legs. She peeped up at her Mama. "I don't like to think about it. It scares me. Who would want to know things before they happen? It's like having to live through it twice. Not once like everyone else."

Addie watched her closely. "You did know you wasn't supposed to marry that man, didn't you? Yet, you went right on and did it. How foolish a girl you are! It's time you are thankful for that gift and use it. It could save you a lot of heartache."

"I told you that it seems like to me that you have to live it twice. Once when you see it in a dream or some other way, and then again when it happens."

Her mother took a deep breath. What she really wanted to do was shake Lottie till her teeth rattled. Why she would go ahead and marry a man she had been warned about was more than Addie could understand? "You wouldn't even have to live it even once, if you had just listened. It don't matter much now. What is done is done. Now you have to pay for yore foolishness.' Addie reached over and pulled Lottie's hair to the side again and shook her head. "That had to hurt, baby girl. It'll take a long time to get its right color back."

"I'll be all right Mama. Don't you worry about me none."

"Didn't Owen plant a tree in the yard at that house that belongs to the Crawford's? The one you all are living in? You know, back when you two first married. There was a storm the week before and blew down that oak tree. Owen dug up a little sapling and brought it and planted right beside where the other one blew down. Do you remember that?"

"What is wrong with yore mind, Mama? What made you go to talking about trees? Did you plum forget what we were talking about?"

Addie turned from the dough she was kneading and looked at Lottie. "I know what I was talking about before, and I know what I am talking about now. My mind is just fine, thank ye. You know what they say about planting a tree, don't ye?"

A look of fear came over Lottie's face. "I most certainly do, now that you reminded me. I can't believe you could even think such a thing."

"And I can't believe you can't think it. When a man plants a tree, when it gets tall enough to shade his grave, he'll die." Addie walked over and pulled Lottie's hair back showing more bruises and also a cut in her temple. "He'll kill you, if something don't kill him first. Men that hit their woman are sorry as a hound dog that won't hunt. And Owen Thompson is a sorry, good-for-nothing excuse for a man."

"Mama! That's my husband you're talking about."

"If he does that to you, what does he do to them poor young'ins of yores? Brody, yore oldest boy, is eight years old and too young to have to do all the working in the fields he has to do. Even if it is just gardening, he ought to be helping with that. You'd think that his family would let him have some time off to raise food for his family. They could give him food from their store. Every time I have been at yore house, there's no enough food in that house to keep a housefly alive. That's why me or yore Papa send food every chance we get. Owen can starve for our part, but we ain't gonna let you nor the children be hungry if we can help it."

"I know Mama. You both are really good to me, but I have to get back before Owen gets home."

"I bet you do little girl. If yore daddy finds out he's hitting you, we may not have to wait for that tree to get large enough to shade his grave for him to die. I'd tell him, but it would just resurrect his feud he has tried years to halt."

Lottie puckered up to cry and ran out the door.

Chapter 8

"Where are you goin' old man?" Addie smiled at the fully dressed Nathe. The day had barely started. It was still dark outside.

"I've got business on Rich Mountain. Think I'll go by Glee's and sees how things look at the old home place."

"I thought it hurt you too much to be in that house, with all the dying that went on there. You haven't been there in years." Addie rubbed her hands together as though she was washing them. Her eyebrows pulled together as she stared at Nathe.

"There are a number of reasons that I need to go there. Glee wants to pay money instead of giving a portion of crops this year. I need to figure out how he's going to get the money. Something ain't right.

"I can't help but think about living there as a boy, about how my life changed because of what happened. With Papa losing his life there and mine skipping away fast, I want to see where Papa drew his last breath. It seems like just yesterday that I played under the apple tree as a little boy. Sometimes I think I smell my Mama's cooking and hear her call my name. I might feel even closer to them there. Life sure has come and gone fast. I need to see the place I was a happy child one more time. I'll try to not think about those sad times when I go."

Addie raised her eyebrows. "Are you sure that is what you want to do? There's a heap of bad memories there. Those might be the ones that come back to you if you go."

"Not sure if I want to or just feel like I *need* to. My life began in that cabin. Mama said it was in the corner by the fireplace. It don't seem that long ago that I played all over that mountain. Hunting. Fishing. Even thoughts of working bring back good memories. My life has been like the steam coming off the pot of coffee on the cookstove, just gone into thin air."

Nathe sat down to tie strips of leather around the toes of the upper part of his shoes to hold them to the soles. Both pieces of leather were ragged.

"You need to make yerself a new pair of shoes. Those are plum wore out." Addie turned and stirred the beans she had put on to cook.

"That would be a waste of time. These will last as long as I need shoes in this life."

Addie wiped her hands on her apron and came and stood in front of Nathe's chair and looked at his back bent over his shoes. "I'm sick and tired of hearing you talk like this. You're acting like you're dying tonight. That doctor don't know nothing for sure. And even he said that you could live a lot longer than others have. You need to decide you're going to fight this here sickness and get better. You have a family that needs you. Stop it! Now do you hear me? Just stop this dying talk. I'm sick of it."

"I wish I didn't have to think about it." Nathe finished tying the leather strings and stood up. "But Amps has been back."

"Yore Grandpa Amps? Did you see him?"

"He came to me first either in a dream or by my bedside. I'm not sure which. But I met him up on Rich Mountain."

"This ain't sounding good. Is something wrong?" Addie sat down in a chair by the table.

"It's this confounded Hooper-Watson feud, I think. Years and years of needless killing and ill will against one or the other. Addie, no disrespect to yore kin, but I've always wanted to believe it was all the Hooper family's fault."

Addie started to speak. Nathe continued, "Shhh. I know better. It could be easy to forget the part my own family played in the bloodshed. You know I've talked to the children. It's like a death grip. For the most part, I thought the talks have been profitable. But Amps appeared to try to warn me of trouble brewing that might prove to require a stronger return than turning the other cheek. Someone is going to do something that will hurt one or both of our families."

Addie wrinkled her forehead as she talked to him. "It just don't seem right to tell you something is about to happen, yet not explain what it is or what you can do about it. Not even who it is that is doing whatever you're talking about. Why did he come? He don't seem to be able to help. Maybe inside he really wants this. Keeping all the trouble stirred up."

Nathe considered it. "Is that what you think? Something inside me says that a dead man wouldn't want to be responsible for stirring up a feud again, but I could be wrong."

"You be careful up there. I take it you think that Glee might have a hand in this."

Nathe wrapped his chin in his right hand and squeezed. "He's the only one of the Hoopers that we have had any dealings with for some time. I guess it could be somebody else, but I have to think it might be him. It may be that I can tell just by talking to him. I'll try to be back tonight. If I can't make it, I'll spend the night with Davie and be back tomorrow." Nathe kissed Addie on the head and left.

xxx

Nathe laid his jaw against the barn and closed his eyes. A tear slid down his cheek. The salty taste of tears and sweat burned a sore on his tongue. He reached out and rubbed a hand against a plank. The wood was rough and smelled of age and decay. Tucker Watson, his Papa, had built this barn when Nathe was almost six years old. With his jaw still against the side of the barn, he opened his eyes and looked down the side. The planks were bowed where nails had rusted, and the wood pulled away from the sides. He's the only other Hooper we talk to these days."

A snort from inside the stable sent hot air against his face and into his ear. He peeked through the crack into the stable, and a mule had his nose pushed against the plank near my head. Its breath smelled of a mixture of corn and hay.

Over forty years had changed Nathe from that little boy that followed close in his Papa's footsteps into a man. Time had seasoned him like it had aged the wood. Things were hard now, not easy like when he was a boy. He longed to hear his Papa call from inside, 'Go feed old Ned'. He wanted once more to hear the sound of the deep voice of Tucker Watson.

"Is something wrong with you?"

The voice caused Nathe to jump back from the barn. "Hello Glee, I was just remembering when I watched my Papa build this barn."

"It needs to be set fire to and a new one built in its place." Glee snurled a lip at the old man.

"This barn is fine. It would help if you nailed some of the boards back down and replaced those that are missing. I can send boards over for you. It could last a long time, if it was taken care of."

"It's *yore* place. You can come and work on it anytime. Just let me know when you'll be here."

"That's not why I came. I was wondering if you still wanted to pay me for the use of the farm with money instead of the crops we agreed upon."

"That's what I said, and you agreed to it. *Yore* money will be ready for you at the end of the month."

"Where are you going to get the money? Are you raising crops that I don't know about and selling them? Making more money that way instead of share cropping? That's not what we agreed on."

Glee's neck turned red and the color moved up into his face. He looked toward Nathe and then quickly away, never letting their eyes meet. "Do I have to answer to you about everything in my life? Where I get my money? What crops I'm growing?"

"I think that is the kind of things I need to be told…about the crops anyway. I want the land to be useful for a long time to come. You have to let it rest once in a while. I'm not against taking the money, if you have it. I'm just concerned how you're going to be able to get money if you're not making a crop." As they talked, Nathe tried to look around for any signs of tilled ground in the fields behind the barn. There was a field of corn just peeking through the dirt, but nothing more.

"This is all hogwash. You're just nosing around to get into my business."

Nathe took a deep breath and tried hard not to fly off the handle. "This is still my land, and my house. I own it all. It's because you are my wife's nephew that I can tolerate you talking such to me. What are you doing that gets you so easily het up about me coming here? Is what you're doing against the law? I need some straight answers. What about that field of corn? What are you going to do with that?"

Glee took a deep breath and seemed calmer. "Do you think I'd do anything against the law, Uncle Nathe? You've known me just about all my life. Haven't I always been a good boy?"

"I have to say you've done nothing, so far, to make me think you are into it with the law, but everything seems to have changed with you. You seem different."

"I ain't changed. You don't see me much anymore. We're all busy with making a living. We don't see family like we used to when I was a boy." Glee reached over and slapped Nathe on the back.

"That's just it. You don't seem busy at all, at least not with things that could get you money. I'm trying real hard to figure out how you're going to pay me."

Glee folded his arms and narrowed his eyes until there was one deep crease across his face. His eyeballs could barely be seen. "I'll pay you with money, like I said. I didn't think when I moved here that you'd be so nosy as to have to know every sort of business that I have. This is my family, and I provide for them without anyone's help. You'll get yore money. How I get it is none of yore business."

The sound of another whinny near the road and clomping of horses' hooves made them both stop and walk to the other side of the barn.

A man sat astride one horse and had the rein to another horse in his hand. "Here's yore horse, sir. The boss sent me over with it. He said to give you this."

Nathe looked at Glee's red face.

Glee grabbed the lead rein. "Thanks. You can be gone now."

"You bought a horse? Where are you getting all this money? And why do you need a mule and a horse? Yore boy is not big enough to help in the fields, at least not old enough to walk behind a horse with a plow. It don't seem you're farming anyway." Nathe grabbed Glee's arm and pulled him around to face him.

Glee jerked back. "Listen, old man, it's none of yore business where I get my money or what I buy."

Nathe clenched and unclenched his fists. "I smell a pole cat. Something ain't right here, and I plan on finding out what it is."

Glee looked directly at Nathe. "Old man, you best just leave me alone and stay off the land. I should be able to live here without yore interference as long as I pay you what I said I would. Get out of here."

Nathe knew it was time to move on. Glee would never tell him what he wanted to know. In fact, he would have already let it go and thought little more about it if I had not warned him. He wished he knew what I appeared to know. The truth was, I knew very little more than he did. I was sent only to warn. Glee, Nathe's children, or any other of the cousins, didn't have much contact with each other, much less time to plan any fighting. But Nathe knew something didn't feel right. There were too many secrets, too much anger for no clear reason.

Nathe was tired. There was nothing to be found out today, but tomorrow was another day. If he left now, he could make it back home just after dark and surprise Addie.

Chapter 9

Two weeks before, the headline in the Tuckasegee Democrat was 'Emigrants Looking For Land To Buy In The Jackson County Area'. It had grabbed Glee's attention. He had read the paper from cover to cover, even though the storekeeper had frowned at him.

It told of business men from Asheville that wanted to acquire logs to be shipped to the northeast where hardwood lumber was needed.' While he was reading the paper at the general store, a man slipped up beside him and told him that he could help him make a considerable amount of money. He could arrange a business with men that had ways to help a man get rich faster than you could shake a stick at. All kinds of businesses. And he could show him how to cut out the middle men. He mentioned logs, land, and moonshine. One venture gave him hope, and he let the man arrange a meeting. Glee now had those men in front of him.

He shook hands with the two men that had arrived on horseback. "I'm glad you gentlemen came."

"You said you wanted to meet with someone about a business, uh, venture in yore letter. That's why we're here."

"That depends if you're willing to work with me."

One man looked around. He pulled Glee closer to a tree. "We have our hands in several ventures. You might need to talk about what you're wanting to supply. We're the men you see in the paper asking for wares in accordance with the law, at least with some of our ventures. Some are legitimate. Some might be on the edges of the law." He looked Glee from head to toe. "You look like you might be willing to help us."

"I got yore name from a man outside the general store in Sylva. I wrote you about what I was willing to do."

"I read that letter, but you might make a little more money if you could provide several things for us instead of just one. We'll give more for yore corn liquor than anybody else that are buying in this area, and surely more money than the government is willing to allow you to make.   The revenue men have moved into the mountains. If a still is not well hid, you'll be shut down and arrested. It needs to be way up into those mountains." He looked at the large mountains all around them.

Glee nodded. "I heard tell about the revenuers over on a mountain near Waynesville. I know somebody fired on the revenuers but missed. That miss was on purpose. We all hunt meat for our families. No good man that hunts for a living and can shoot a squirrel from a tree easy enough would ever miss a full-grown man. They won't stay around here long looking for stills."

"So you think he missed him on purpose? That may be so, but it's a dangerous enterprise, but a smart man like yoreself could stay hidden. Isn't that right?" He poked his friend in the ribs and winked at Glee.

Glee felt sick. This was not going the way he'd hoped. He'd made the agreement with Nathe about a yearly pay off. He'd bought another horse to pull heavy loads. What if all his plans failed?

"They'll never find me, but I talked about other things that I'm willing to do for you. Are you buying such as I mentioned in my letter?" Glee swallowed and then fed them his lie. "I tell you my land is way up in the mountains. I can supply you that without worrying about revenuers or breaking the law."

"It all depends if it's worth our time. We have plenty of buyers for such things in Asheville and even further north. How many loads can you supply a week?"

"A week? I was thinking maybe one a month?"

The men looked at each other and laughed. The older man looked back to Glee and stopped smiling. "So have you wasted our time coming down here? There's lots of money to be made, if

you are willing to stick yore neck out a little further
and work a little harder."

"I'm not interested in putting my life on the
line, but I'm not wasting yore time. I didn't realize
that you wanted the supply that often. I can do it.
I'm sure I can. When would I need to have the first
load ready for you? What are you willing to give
per load?"

They quoted Glee a price much more than he
had hoped for. He kept a straight face and tried to
not smile or appear too anxious. He knew life was
going to get better from here on out.

Glee noted the men's finely tailored suits.
They looked just like the pictures he had seen in a
book laying on the counter at the general store in
Sylva. The catalog was Sears and Roebuck. It
had over five-hundred pages in it filled with
clothes, pocket watches, and about anything else a
person could think of. And some things he didn't
know anyone had thought of before.

One of the Asheville men had brown breeches
with a checkered shirt. His little felt hat looked
like it had been dyed in the same lot as his clothes.
The other man had a dark black mustache, much
darker than his thinning hair. His breeches were
black and his coat had a long tail, but the front was
short and stuck out longer at his waist. Underneath
his coat was a crisp white shirt and a gray vest. His
shirt had a collar that stood straight up and buttons
that fastened so tight around his neck that his face
stayed red the whole time they talked. Both men's
shoes were made of leather that had been worked
on till they had a shine so big that a man could see

himself in them. These were the best clothes money could buy, he figured. Someday Glee planned to dress like that.

Glee looked down at his own clothes. He figured that the men would be dressed well, and he had tried to look business like. But right now he felt shabby. He reached for the sides of his coat and pulled them together in front. They didn't quite meet. When he reached to shake their hand, his sleeve came halfway to the elbow. The right cuff showed loose stitching that opened wide enough to show his wrist beneath. To shake the second man's hand, he had to raise himself up from the wagon seat. He put his foot on the front of the wagon to steady himself. His handmade shoes were worn and tied to his foot with thin leather strips of dried deer hide.

The difference in their lives was pretty plain, but someday he knew he'd be as successful as them.

The men looked at Glee and tried to gauge if he was able to supply them with what they needed. They must have been satisfied because they smiled, and the older gentleman shook his hand a little harder and longer. "Tell me when we'll meet."

Glee looked to see if anyone was watching or listening. He lowered his voice to just above a whisper.

"I'll have the first load out to you in about a week. Is that acceptable?"

"One of my men will come to yore place this time next week, if you will just supply us directions."

Glee shook his head. "No. I need to meet you somewhere off the mountain. Somewhere no one will see us."

The man narrowed his eyes. "Do you have others that you are giving yore business? I want to know who I'm bidding against. I need to be the only one in this area that you work with."

"No it's not that. Uh…uh….I thinks it's best to meet off the mountain. Don't want yore men messing up these nice wagons you have by coming up that big mountain. As for whispering, I don't want nobody horning in on my deal."

"Very well. Give me directions."

"I have all the turns written up for you. It's not far off the main road in Tuckasegee." Glee handed him a paper.

The man looked over the directions. "I may send them down early to make a trial run on this road. They need to know exactly what the road is like, and they need to make sure there is no mistake in picking up the load. They'll have yore money at the first pick up."

"Yes sir." Glee watched them leave. He felt richer already.

xxx

Back at home, Glee grabbed his wife and swung her around.

She giggled. "What's got into you? You look like the cat that caught the bird."

"I feel like things are about to change in our life. Things are going to go good for a change."

She looked worried. "What are you talking about?"

"Woman, I am going to take you places. " He poked a finger at the hole in her dress. "You won't have to dress in rags much longer. I will buy you ready made clothes from catalogs. No! I will take you to some high falutin' store in the city and let you pick them out yoreself."

She turned bright red. "What are you talking about? We can't even buy material so I can hand-make a new dress. You sound like a crazy man."

"We'll be rich enough to leave this mountain and never come back."

She turned back to the potatoes she was peeling. "I don't want to leave this mountain, unless it's to go up to Waynesville nearer to my family."

"We can do that, but I am thinking up north where there's high fashion and pretty homes. Maybe over near the ocean. You can buy ready canned food. Neither of us will have to work or beg for every morsel of food we eat."

His wife grinned and hugged him. She would love to be near her mama and papa.

"I will make this money and be gone, and they'll never know when we left."

She swallowed and took her arm down from around his neck. "It's not against the law what you are going to do, is it? I don't want no man of mine in prison. We have a son to think about. Glee, don't do nothing foolish."

Glee stared at her and walked out the door, his mind already thinking of how to be able to supply a load a week.

XXX

Owen left his house just as the sun rose with a red glow, but the sky was quickly covered by a dark cloud. The day looked like it might be stormy by the time he got off the mountain.

Lottie thought he had gone to work. She would find out soon enough that he didn't. But he wanted...no, he needed...to get out of the house and off that mountain, somewhere away from the children and Lottie. She'd been sweet when they first met. It had been easy to get her to like him. She had looked at him like he hung the moon back then.

Her parents hated him now. That was why he made sure she didn't go over there much. Her Mama was strange. She looked at him with an evil eye, and he felt she put spells on him. No matter what he did, she'd have a saying or silly notion why he shouldn't be doing it.

Lottie took up for her Mama and Papa against him. He hated himself when he acted like he did sometimes, but Lottie made him hit her to get her attention and make her do what he said. His Mama always did what his Papa said and had as long as he could remember. Why did Lottie have to be any different?

Bad Blood 81

Chapter 10

It felt like fate when Owen met Glee that day. Glee was dressed up like he was going to Sunday meeting, and it was just Tuesday. There was a smile on his face from ear to ear.

"Howdy Glee. You sure look happy."

"I am happy. Things are going my way. And it's about time too. All I need is to find a person or two that'll work for me, and I'll be on my way to having more money than any man in these mountains. I might move up to Asheville. Shoot I might move up to Virginia and get me a big farm and raise…"

Owen stopped him. "Did you say you're looking to hire somebody? If so, I might be available. I could probably get work on some farm, but I'm not cut out for farming. My hands would have all kinds of blisters and rough places on them. I grew up doing easier work. Would you like to hire me?"

"Don't you still work for yore papa at the general store? Besides, this is not easy work either. You would more than likely get a blister working for me as well."

"My Papa thinks that I should learn what it's like to work hard, so he fired me and won't hire me back. Working at his store was hard. I unloaded supplies at the depot that came in by train and then brought them in the wagon to the store. Then I unloaded them again and put them on the shelves. He wanted me to work from the time the sun came up till it went down at that store. The day I fussed about that, he told me, 'Go make a living for yore family where you really have to work hard. Then you'll appreciate a job like this one.' Cut me right off. Lottie thinks I still work there. It's been three weeks now. She started the garden. I come to town every day like I'm going to work. Sure glad I ran into you. Pretty soon she'll figure out there ain't no money coming in anymore."

Glee laughed. This had done everything Glee and the other Hoopers could have wanted to happen to Nathe Watson. Glee reached his hand out toward Owen.

Owen reached his hand out to meet Glee's. "So are you going to hire me?"

Glee shook his hand but said, "You think store keeping and farming is hard, you'll find out this may be harder than anything you ever did. But if you start, you have to promise me you won't quit me till I've made the money that I need to get out of these mountains."

"Well at least it's a job. I promise. Right now beggars can't be choosers. Do we start today?"

Glee gave a jerk on Owen's arm and pulled him into the wagon. "You just have to keep it all quiet. I don't want nobody trying to get in on this business. I want it all for myself. If you say one word, you won't like what I would do to you."

Owen looked at Glee and laughed, but the look on Glee's face was serious.

"I mean it, Owen. One word, and you're a dead man. The reason I'm hiring you is that I'm desperate, and I have enough stories on you, that if I told them, Lottie's Papa and brothers would do the killing for me. My threats are real. I think you've heard enough about either one of our families to know that we don't make threats and not carry 'em out."

xxx

Addie had one side of the tub, and Sugar had the other. Inside were three pounds of flour and three pounds of meal. Nathe had cut a block off a hog's jowl, wrapped it in paper, and stuck it inside. There were two cans of beans and a can of sausage patties. Sugar had looked at her Mama and started to say something when Addie put in the last of the loaf of souse. It was her favorite, but she knew Lottie needed it more. Addie had sliced the souse and then tied a string around it to pull it back into a loaf to keep it from drying out. She put the tub on the back porch. They had left right after breakfast to take it to Lottie.

Lottie had not seen them yet. They set the tub down so they could catch their wind and watched her as she stirred lye soap into the steaming water. A pile of clothes lay behind her waiting to be washed. She would stir a while then cut strips off the stick of wood and poke in the flames below the iron pot.

"Lottie, where are them babies?"

"Mama, what are you doing here?" Lottie kept glancing at the tub that was covered with a cloth. "You scared me half to death when you spoke. They're shelling corn out in the crib. I let them do an ear every once in a while and hide some seed so we will have some to plant. It's nearly planting time, and I think we might be able to get a small patch of corn planted with the seed I've saved."

Lottie looked at the tub again. "What have you got there, Mama? Is it for me?"

The children heard the voices and came running. No asking for them. They jerked up the cloth and their eyes widened. "It's food. Real good food, too." Brody reached in and pulled the string and grabbed a slice of souse and ran.

"Get back here, Brody Thompson. I didn't say you could have that."

"Let him have it, Lottie. He looked hungry." Sugar had tears in her eyes. She reached down and pulled out another piece of the souse and gave it to August, who sat down in the dust and started to eat.

Addie pushed her lips together as long as she could, but it had to be said. "Where is that sorry Owen? I heard he ain't working for his family and hasn't in quite a while. That is why I brought the food."

"He's been working the last few weeks. There ain't been no pay yet, but he got him a real job with Glee."

"With Glee? What is Glee doing that he needs help with?"

"I don't rightly know, but he's going to pay for him to help. Owen won't talk about it with me."

"You don't think they are making 'shine do you? Surely that sorry nephew of mine wouldn't do that. If he is, I'll get him out of yore Papa's home-place so fast it will make his head swim."

"I wouldn't think they are making 'shine. Somebody would have to be growing some corn, and according to Davie, they ain't made much in the way of crops up there in a couple of years. But, it's possible I suppose." Lottie wrinkled her forehead and thought real hard. "Don't y'all get half of whatever they grow...sharecropping and all? Have they given you any corn?"

"Nathe also talks like Glee ain't much of a farmer. We hadn't seen no corn, not to say they ain't just keeping it for themselves. About all we've seen from his attempt at work are some apples and few taters last fall. I figured they're letting Marshall and the wife's family keep them up, growing their food and even canning it for them. Otherwise, they'd have starved by now. How in tarnation do they pay somebody to do nothing? Where does his money come from? What are they doing?"

Lottie looked at her tub of food. "I really do work hard, Mama. I know I shouldn't be taking food from you all, but it sure looks good."

"Of course you should take food from us. I wasn't talking about you. You do the best you can with what little you got. I'm talking about that little man you call a husband. He makes you and the children work too hard. If I could see some sort of help coming from him, I wouldn't talk about him so bad. I know it's hard times, and you say he's working, but I never seen you getting any benefit from it. Does he drink it up?"

Lottie drug the tub to the edge of the porch and started to unpack it. "You can take yore tub back. I thank you for the food. When my garden comes in, I'll try to pay you back for some of this."

Addie put her hands on her hips. "I don't want you to pay me back. I want you and the children to have food to eat. You're my child and I love you."

Lottie swallowed hard and nodded. "I know. Thank you."

"Come on, Sugar. Let's get home before dark. I need to be doing our washing, too." She turned to Lottie. "Come when you can. You need to send word if you ever get this low on food again. Do you hear me?"

Lottie opened her mouth.

"Don't you open yore mouth and lie. Don't deny that you had no food in that house of yores. Yore children tearing into that food the way they did told it all."

"Ok, Mama. I'll let you know." She held her stomach with her hand.

"You're eating for two so don't let them have all the food. Eat some yurself. But you can hide it from that sorry man of yores."

"Mama!"

"Come on Sugar. Let's go."

Chapter 11

Beck finished plowing and brought the horse
to the barn. He went to the corn crib and pulled out
a dozen ears, shucked the corn, and pushed his
thumb against the kernels. The first ones fell with
a ding when they hit the bucket below him. Old
Dan, the big stout bay that Nathe owned, had
worked hard all day. It needed some grain and hay
too.

The water sloshed onto his dusty pants. Beck
raised the bucket and poured water into a trough in
Dan's stall.

Nathe stood at the opening of the barn and
watched him. "I just came from looking over the
field. You did a good job today. It would've taken
me three days to do what you did in one. I'm sure
glad you agreed to work for me this summer."

"Glad to have a job. I came back to Jackson
County because my Papa's brother was dying, and

I felt they needed me. When he passed on, I couldn't leave until I was sure my aunt would be fine without me. She's doing good, but it'll help for me to be here this summer. She don't need to be alone right now. That widower neighbor plans to help her get the crops into the ground and help with the harvest."

Nathe handed a bucket to Beck. "I know yore aunt's house is past my son-in-law's and daughter Lottie's house. Would you mind to stop by and give this milk to her? She had a newborn baby to die about three months ago. She just found out she's in the family way again. Their cow went dry week before last. She and those children need milk to drink."

Beck took the bucket. "I'll be glad to. It's not out of my way atall. I remember seeing Lottie the first time when she was about this high." He held his hand level to his waist. "Back when I came for visits with my Papa and Mama."

"She's all grown up, faster than I wanted her to. She married Owen Thompson a few years ago. She wasn't much more than in her teens. Too young for him. That's neither here nor there. What's done is done. I'll see you tomorrow, then."

"I'll be here by 6:00 in the morning. Get a start on the planting. The quicker we get seed in the ground, the sooner you'll get a harvest."

xxx

Lottie took the clean clothes off the wooden fence on the porch where she had put them to dry.

Piece by piece, she folded them. She laid them in the chair by the door. She didn't hear the man walk up and jumped when he spoke to her.

"Lottie Watson?" He took off his hat and held it in his hands as he talked to her.

Lottie stopped folding clothes and looked at the man. "Lottie Thompson now, but, yes, I was once Lottie Watson. Who are you?"

"You don't recognize me? Of course when I saw you last you were eleven years old. I was sixteen. I was here that summer visiting cousins. I noticed back then you were growing up. You were big for eleven. Every fall we'd visit here after we got in our harvest. We'd come to see my father's brother."

Lottie stared at him and leaned her head to the side as she searched in her memory. Her eyes lit up. "Beckley Radford. I wouldn't have recognized you if I'd met you in the road. You're a man all grown now."

"I've spent a few years logging, and then I worked on the road that goes over the mountain to Tennessee. Both of those jobs will either kill you or make a man of you. It did the latter. I'm surprised you remembered me atall."

"Well, all the older girls thought you hung the moon back then, including my older sister. I was just beginning to notice the boys. I knew you'd not look at me twice. I was too young and ugly."

"You were young, but never ugly."

Lottie blushed and put her hands to her mouth and covered her smile.

Seven year old Brody came to the edge of the porch and asked, "Mama, who is this man?"

"This here is a man I knew when he was just a boy and I was a young girl. His name is Beck."

Brody looked at him from head to toe and then back at his Mama. "What does he want?"

Lottie looked at Beck and then at the bucket in his hand.

"This here is for you. Yore Papa sent it. I'm working for him this planting season. He ain't well it seems."

"That's true. He's very poorly."

Beck looked at Brody. "Yore Grandpa knew my Papa, and he even remembered me from when I was a child." Beck turned back to Lottie. "I told him that I remembered you when he hired me."

"If Papa knew yore family, then he must think highly of them to hire you." She looked again at the bucket in his hand. "What did he send me?"

"Milk. For you and the babies he said."

Lottie smiled. "Papa is so good to me. I don't know what I'll do if something happens to him. He makes sure I have everything I need."

"I thought that was a husband's duty, to take care of his wife and children."

Lottie blushed. "Oh, he does. He tries hard, but it seems we just never have enough. There are a lot of people in that same pickle around here. It's hard to make ends meet." Lottie took the bucket. She took a clean cloth off the stack she had folded and tied it as a cover over the top of the pail. She handed it to Annie May. "Take this up to the spring house and put it in the cold water. You or Brody can go back and get it when it's time for supper tonight."

She smiled at Beck. "Much obliged for bringing it to me. I don't get over to Mama's and Papa's as much as I'd like."

"You're welcome." Beck stood at the edge of the porch. He leaned to the side and looked behind Lottie and saw eyes peeping around the door. "I see you have a little one in there."

August sat in the floor where Lottie had placed the table leg on her dress tail so she would not run off. "Oh, that's August. I had Annie May tending to her sister. She's neart two. She's a handful and will run off if you don't watch her every minute."

Annie May showed a corn shuck doll to her baby sister.

"You have yoreself a house full of youngins, don't ye?"

Lottie smiled. "I reckon. They sure do make my life happy. Would you like to rest a spell before you leave?"

"That'd be real nice. I'll just sit here on the step while you finish folding yore washing." He laid his hat to the side and raked at this thick, dark, curly hair.

Lottie folded a shirt of Owen's as she talked. "You worked on the road that goes across the mountain to White Oak Flats, you say? Do you have a family? Maybe a wife or children there. Or did you bring them with you to live here?"

"I had a family in Tennessee at one time. I thought I could make good money logging, so I worked and went home about every three months or so to the wife and kids. I left right after my Mama and Papa died. It hurt bad losing them. When I came home last time, my wife had packed up and moved her and the children down to South

Carolina where her family lived. She left me a letter explaining why she had left. I wrote and tried to get them to come back, but they wouldn't. That was a few years back. Then, I worked on the road over the mountain. I came to North Carolina because my Papa's brother was dying. I wanted to see if my aunt needed anything. Thought I might stay around for the summer to make sure she can make it on her own."

"I guess you'll go down to South Carolina to be with yore wife when the time comes?"

"Don't think so. The wife told me there was no need for me to come down there."

Lottie took in a sharp breath. "What about yore children?"

"I went down there to get them once. She caught me and beat me out of the house with a broom. My oldest son begged to come with me, but she made me realize I couldn't work and tend to him. So, I left him and the others with her. I guess I didn't think that through before I left. I just missed them so bad."

"That's just horrible. Poor babies without their Papa. You seem like you would be a good Papa, too."

"I tried to be. And a good husband too. Don't rightly know why she left. I know I wasn't around a lot, but it was because I was trying to make a living for them."

Lottie finished folding and stared at Beck. "How many children do you have?"

Beck looked into the distance. "There are two boys and two girls. Don't guess I'll ever see them again. Not unless they come looking for me someday." He stopped and looked at Lottie who had tears in her eyes at his sad story. "Well, I'd better mosey on towards home. It was nice to see you again."

Neither of them saw the man come up and slip behind the side of the house out of their sight. He leaned against the logs, watching and listening to the last few words of their talk.

Chapter 12

Lottie pulled the bean pot from the heat onto the ledge of the warmer of the stove. "Brody, run out to the spring and get that bucket of milk for supper. Do it right now, before yore Papa gets here."

"Let Annie May get it. She took it up there."

"That's the very reason I said for you to go and get it."

Brody stomped off the back porch and slammed the door.

The backdoor creaked as it opened. Lottie spun around. "Brody Thompson, get up…" She found herself face to face with Owen. His breath smelled of hard liquor, and his eyes were streaked with red.

"It's me, yore loving husband. Brody did as he was told. Too bad you can't do the same."

Lottie took the cloth she had used to pull the beans from the heat and threw it on the table. "What are you talking about?"

"I told you to not be having no company or to be goin' anywhere when I'm gone. You don't listen to me any better than the children do to you. I guess Brody gets that from you, don't you think? "

"I ain't brought no company into this house." She stared at him. "Why are you drunk? Are you spending all our money on 'shine? We need that there money. We're out of most everything. Coffee, sugar, flour. I thought you were going to bring me money tonight, so I could go to the store and get some staples for cooking."

"You ain't concerned about food. You're just trying to change our talk so I won't ask about that man you was entertaining a bit earlier."

"I didn't entertain no gentleman today, or any other day."

"Don't say that to me. I saw him. He brought you something from yore Papa."

"Oh. That was a man that works for Papa. He brought milk for me and the children to drink. I wasn't entertaining him. If you know so much, you'd know that."

"Brought milk, did he? Just for you all? Not for me?"

"Well, of course, it's for you too. Papa knows these children need milk and, with me in the family way, he thinks I should be drinking milk, so I'll have enough milk to nurse the baby when it gets here."

"One excuse is as good as another when you are covering up a sin. There was no need for him to stay as long as he did, if he just brought something. He was here quite a while."

Lottie put her hands on her hips. "I'm not covering up no sins. I ain't sinned, none at all. Nothing happened but milk passing from one hand to another. That's all. He wasn't here long at all." She walked away and started to set the table.

Owen took two long strides, jerked Lottie around, and looked down into her face. "You don't fuss with me. I have to believe what my own two eyes saw and what my two ears heard. Y'all was talking all lovey dovey about him living without his wife and kids. Do you think you want a man that leaves his wife and children to fend for themselves? He'd leave you, too. Not work hard like me to make a living and stay right here with you while I do it. You think you want him?"

"I don't want no man, not ever again. You're acting crazy. It's that liquor that's talking. You can eat, and then go and sleep it off."

Owen grabbed her arm and twisted it behind her. He walked her backward to the wall and leaned all the strength of his body against hers until she could barely breathe. "Stay away from him. You'd better not see him again. Do you hear me?"

She gasped for air. "I hear you."

He leaned back and threw her against the table.

Lottie looked at her wrists and watched the redness turn purple. It would be black by tomorrow.

Owen walked to the bed. He pulled off his
shoes, fell on the covers, and was soon snoring.

Lottie fed the children and put them to bed.
She lay down with Annie May and August and
slept.

xxx

Lottie built a fire the next morning, but Owen
slept on. He woke up as Lottie was putting biscuits
into the oven. He brought his shoes to the table
and sat down to put them on. Lottie slipped out the
door without speaking. The sun was still hidden
behind the mountain but gave enough light that you
could make out the shapes of the trees. Inside the
hen house, she felt under three hens and got five
eggs in all. Back inside the house, she pulled a
skillet to the heat to fry his eggs. Owen acted like
nothing had happened.

He came and stood behind her and looked over
her shoulder. "Good morning, Wife. You about
got my breakfast ready?"

"It's almost done." She didn't look up.

He reached around her and pulled her around
and against his chest. "Do you remember the first
time you saw me?"

She shook her head yes.

"I told you back then that I wouldn't abide a
wife that tried to make me jealous."

Lottie felt sick at her stomach. "I wasn't
trying to make you jealous. I didn't do anything."

"I hate a liar. Do you think this man is better
looking than me? Tell me how you described me
to yore friends when we first met. Tell it like you
told me back then."

She had to make him think she was all gooey eyed for him like she used to be. "I told them, 'His face is long and angular, strong and purposeful. His eyebrows all but hide his dark blue eyes that pierce and excite even the quietest of girls, especially me.' He stared at her with his mouth partly open, waiting for her to continue.

"I told them you looked at me like you knew all about me. You looked deep in my soul and picked up on my interest long before I even knew it was there." She had memorized all this, because every time after he was mean, he would get up the next morning and do this same thing. If she talked it up to him, just right, he would leave her alone for a while. She had to make him feel that she still felt that same way about him.

He jerked her to his chest and squeezed her tight. He raised his eyebrows and tilted his head.

"I invited you to a taffy pull, and you came."

"There was more to it than that, and you know it." He laughed and pushed her away from him.

She heard August whimper. She shushed Owen. "We'll wake the children if we don't quiet down. You sit and eat while I go and get some water for cooking beans for tonight."

Once outside, Lottie threw up.

She grabbed a bucket and threw out the water from the half-full bucket. She needed to get away, and drawing a bucket of water was a reasonable way of hiding till Owen left.

xxx

Owen ate his breakfast and left before Lottie came back. He felt satisfied that he had left her with the feelings that he was the only man for her.

Chapter 13

Glee was asleep and awakened to a loud noise. The sound came from the table as it fell sideways and onto the floor. He tried to jump up but tangled himself up in the cover. He fell by the side of the bed.

The table was a good solid one that sat on four legs just under the window on the north side of the house. There was no reason for it to fall, but there it lay. The oil lamp had broken into pieces, and there was a sickly smell of coal oil. His wife and boy had gone to her Mama's in Waynesville for a week. He was thankful she was not here to have heard that.

The sky was still dark when Glee slid the wooden lock back and jerked open the door to look outside. It was probably about midnight as the moon had been topping the mountain when he had gone to bed, and now it was above the trees. He'd been asleep no more than two hours he figured.

He stood in the door and listened. There was nothing other than a hoot owl in the distance and the shriek of a bobcat in the valley behind the barn. No sound of horse's hooves. No running footsteps. Nothing. "Anybody out there?" He cocked his head to the side and listened. "Make yerself known or get yerself shot, one or the other." There was no movement or sound.

Glee came inside and slid the lock back into place. He walked the floor and finally lit a lantern and stood by the door. There was still no sound outside, so he went back out. It had rained hard the day before, and the yard was muddy. If anyone had been by the window, there would be footprints below it.

He held the lantern low down to the ground. The mud was smooth. His own footprints were all that were seen in any direction. His heart beat hard against his ribs.

Inside again, he picked up the table and turned it upside down. He shook each leg to see if it was loose and wobbly. Each was as tight as a tick. He set it up on all fours and shook it again. It was as sturdy as the day he had repaired it the week after they moved in. The table had been lying on the front porch. One leg had been pulled from the notch that held it to a flat board for the top. It was easy to make it a sturdy and useable again. He hadn't been able to figure why anyone would want to leave such a good table behind. Someone had taken great pains to make it. There were even notches in each leg to fancy it up. It looked like it had been stained with crushed walnut hulls. But

Watsons were funny people. You never knew what
was going on in their minds. Glee figured if they
didn't want it, he'd take it as his own.

There had been little things happen since he
and the wife had moved in that he couldn't explain,
but nothing like this. He had woken one night to a
voice moaning but had laid it to a bobcat, although
it sounded like a man wailing and crying. Another
night he had come in late and the wife had sworn
she could hear a child crying.

He placed the table back underneath the
window. This made him want to rethink taking it
with him if he was ever able to move away from
this mountain. No, not IF, but WHEN. Some
way, somehow, he was getting away from here.
He needed a way to make money to buy his own
place. Somewhere away from this end of Jackson
County. Maybe up near Waynesville, way closer
to his wife's people.

Glee lay back on the bed, this time with his
clothes on. He needed to sleep but he felt shaky
inside, a little scared if he had to admit it. A good,
four-legged table doesn't fall over on its own.

His eyes closed as he drifted into sleep, but
jerked open at the sound of tap, tap, tap. It
sounded like someone was beating a post into the
ground outside. The sound was in rhythm of a man
that drew back a hammer and let it fall on the post.
Then it sounded more like three people. Each
separate hit was just a second or two behind the
other…a few seconds of raising the hammer and
then three hits fell again.

Glee grabbed the gun from the corner and jerked open the door so hard it crashed against the wall. The sounds stopped as soon as he stepped outside.

"Who's out here? I hear you doing something. Now come on out so I can see who you are." No one made a sound. "Get on out here, or I'll shoot."

Glee raised the shotgun to his shoulder and aimed it just over the barn. The sound echoed for miles. "Next time I won't miss. Show yerself."

Everything was quiet. He went back into the house and bolted it. Glee leaned against the door and breathed slow, deep breaths. He gripped the gun tight and waited. There were no more sounds of tapping. The table was still upright where he had set it earlier. His breathing eased, and his heart settled to a regular beat in his chest. He sat down in a chair beside the bed and laid his gun across his knees. He would nod off but quickly opened his eyes as his head jerked, over and over again until the sun cast a red glow in the east.

Glee put the shotgun back in the corner. He swept up the broken glass from the lamp, and sopped up some of the coal oil. He opened the window to let the air help dry up the rest. It all seemed like a bad dream.

He went to the old chest that his Papa had given him when his Grandpa Clay had died. Inside, just under the family Bible, laid a pistol. He took it out and carried it to the bed. From now on, he would sleep with the gun under his pillow. Just in case.

Glee heard my laughter, and he jerked the covers over his head.

XXX

Glee looked around before he harnessed the horse. Everything was just like it was the night before. He didn't even own a good hammer. He had his Papa's, but the handle was broken. He opened the tack room door, and the hammer head was lying behind the horse collar.

Everything has an explanation, he thought. But tables falling over by themselves? No explanation. Someone driving wood into the ground? That was what it sounded like. But the daylight showed no footprints of man or animal.

The trip to Webster gave Glee time to think about all that happened last night. Most things that happen in the darkness of the night seem different in the light of day. This did not! He couldn't explain it. Haints was the best he could come up with.

Chapter 14

Sugar sat the bushel of beans in the floor and flopped in a kitchen chair. Lottie didn't turn around but continued to wash the jars readying them for canning.

"Mama said to tell you these need canning as soon as you can. She picked them yesterday, and they will be hard to string if you wait another day."

Lottie nodded and kept washing the same jar over and over.

Sugar yelled, "Hey, did you hear me? Don't just nod yore head at me. I took the trouble to bring them over to you, the least you can do is act like you know I am here."

"Thanks Sugar. I appreciate it." Lottie's back heaved in a hiccup motion. Her voice sounded like her tongue was thick.

"What's wrong with you? Are you crying?"

Lottie shook her head hard from side to side. "I'm just fine. Now get on home, and help Mama."

With one grab and quick pull, Sugar pulled Lottie around to face her. "Lordy, Lottie. What in tarnation happened to yore lip?"

Lottie's lip was rolled almost inside out. "I fell out on the porch this morning. Hit my lip on the step."

"You're a liar, a crazy liar. That no good Owen hit you."

Lottie put up her hand trying to stop Sugar from talking. "You don't know nothing. I told you I fell. You have to believe what I tell you."

Sugar narrowed her eyes. "I don't believe liars once theys commence to lying. It comes natural once they get the hang of it. You ain't never done nothing but lie for that man since he took to beating you. You think everybody is not talking about you, but they are. They all know there ain't a person alive that falls as much as you say you do. It's pretty plain that man is a good for nothing..."

"Stop it right there Sugar. That's my husband you're talking about. I love him, and I don't want nobody talking about him."

Sugar got up in Lottie's face. "Well, you're my sister, and I don't want nobody hitting on you. So there. That makes us even, now don't it." She jerked around and sat back down. "When are you going to get up enough nerve to leave that man. He don't love you, or he wouldn't hit on you the way he does. Why can't you see that? He's as sorry as the day is long. Does he beat on the kids too?"

Lottie was slow to answer, and Sugar knew it was worse than she had thought. "The children are lazy sometimes. He just tries to beat the lazy out of them. He don't mean to be so hard on them. If they'd be still and take it, there wouldn't be so many bruises."

"You're as crazy as he is, if you put up with that. A good spanking shouldn't be leaving many bruises." Sugar took a deep breath and talked calmer. "You do know that one of these days he's going to kill you or one of the kids, just like old man Judson killed his wife."

"You don't know that he killed her. No law said he did."

"Of course he killed her. She came to church every Sunday with bruises just like YOU. Always falling, she said. We were just kids, but back then you were as sure as I was that he was beating her. Just like Owen does, he walked into church right by her side and nodded his head when she told everyone about falling when she was getting ready for church, daring anyone to say different. Now, you want to act like you believed them. Don't that tell you anything? Lottie, get away from this man. Take yore children and run."

Lottie sat down across from Sugar and rocked back and forth in her chair. They stared at each other. Then Lottie's lips puckered up in a tight wad, her swollen lip purple on the underside, and she squeezed her eyes shut. Tears ran down her cheeks. She whispered, "I can't leave him. He would track me down and kill me. He told me so." She grabbed the slop bucket and puked in it.

Sugar stood up and ran to her sister's side. "How do you let that man touch you? You having this baby is another string to tie you to him. No doubt that's what he figures they're good for."

"Don't talk about my babies like that. They're not strings. I love them with all my heart. I'd do anything for them. "

"Is that true? Would you leave this good-for-nothing so theys can be safe? Are you really going to do that? Because that is what they and you need. If you'll do anything for them, get them out of here."

Lottie leaned back in the chair, pushing it back until it stood on the back two legs. She leaned her head against the wall. "I don't know how. There's no place to run. Where do you think I should go? Who in their right mind is going to take in me and these babies?"

Sugar went to the screen door and looked out at the rotten floor along the edge of the porch. Further out, the door of the smoke house hung sideways, swinging on one hinge. She turned and looked around the room. Every stick of furniture in there, their Papa and Mama had given her. Nothing came from Owen or his family. The table and chairs, the rocker, the cookstove and poker set by the fireplace. The skillets and dishes. The cornshuck pallets on the floor for the children, she and Mama had made when the third baby was born. Lottie's and Owen's bed. Even the slop jar under the edge of the bed was the one she had at their house when they were growing up. It had set under the girl's bed just like it did under Lottie's now. The exact same place…beside the leg at the head of the bed. Mama had given it to her, now that the rest of us were bigger and could go to the outhouse in the night, if we needed to.

Lottie watched Sugar. "What are you looking for?"

"I am thinking about yore house and the things in it. Nothing important." Sugar strained a smile and looked Lottie in the eyes. "I love you sister. I don't know where you could go. I'm not sure what I would do, but I think I would find a way to get out of here and take my children with me. Living on the streets of Asheville can't be any worse than living like this." She hugged Lottie and left.

Chapter 15

Glee rubbed his face. He needed to get one more man to work for him. He and Owen could not get the loads out by themselves. He had promised the men from the company three loads a week. Two was the best he and Owen could do alone. The only place he could put out the word for help without it getting back to Nathe was where men were working on the railroad from Waynesville to Murphy. He hoped to hire someone today. If he failed to get the business men what they wanted on time, the contract was no good.

There was a foreman every fifty yards. The man nearest him stood with the butt of the gun sitting on his foot and one hand on the barrel.

"Do you have any people looking for jobs coming by? I need to hire someone."

The man looked over at the men that worked a few feet from him. "These men are prisoners. They'd probably love to work for you." He laughed so hard his shoulders shook. "But then I'd have to shoot them as they ran away."

Glee face flushed. "So you don't have men working that are not prisoners?"

"Naw. Just prisoners."

"It seems they'd be hard to keep in line working outside like this." The men eyed Glee. One spit toward him, and the guard turned the gun toward him. He went back to work.

"We got plenty of them we bring down from Asheville. They like the outside work as opposed to staying in the cells all day. But we do have a runaway once in a while. One did it yesterday. One of my best workers, too. I shot at him, but don't think I hit him. Couldn't leave the rest of them to hunt him down, but they're sending down some men to find him. He won't be loose for long. The privilege for working on the railroad won't be his ever again."

Glee raised his hand in a wave and left.

A mile away, while crossing a creek, Glee heard, "Psstt. Did I hear you say you need to hire someone?"

"Yes, but where did you hear that?" Glee glanced back toward where the guard and prisoners had been.

"An acquaintance heard you telling that guard. I've been following you since you left the railroad."

Ann Robbins Phillips

Glee looked behind the man and scratched his head. "Are you that prisoner that escaped?"

The man looked at Glee's hand that lay on his rifle. "I'm an innocent man. I need to make some money and get back to my family in the north. I could live in yore barn, maybe. I'm a good worker."

It was not the way Glee had hoped things would go, but he didn't have much choice, if he wanted to get another load out on time. "As you are so good following and keeping up, you follow me home. Stay far enough back that, if we meet someone, they won't know you are with me. Don't speak. I don't want anyone seeing us together. This job may not last more than a month or two at best. Staying in my barn is not possible, but there is a barn down the mountain a little ways. It's an old home place. The house has fallen in, but the barn will give some shelter."

"Thanks…"

"Just call me Glee. That's all you need to know. I'll show you the place. Stay out of sight while you're staying there. There's a house out the road a ways from it. Don't let the people there see you. Before the sun rises, you leave and stay on the road that goes up the mountain. Come up until you reach my place. Don't be late. We have a lot of work to do."

"What exactly will we be doing?"

"I'll show you tomorrow morning. Be at my house at the first light of the day."

xxx

By the time Glee had fed the horse that night, he was too tired to do much but fall into bed. Inside the house, he looked to make sure the window was closed above the table. He shut the door and bolted it. The wind from the door blew the curtain. He jerked his shoes off and lay down across the bed until he fell asleep.

It was near midnight when Glee opened his eyes, but he didn't dare move. Just behind him he could hear the sound of something dragging across the bare wooden floor. His hand slid carefully out from his side and under the pillow. The cold metal slipped into his hand, and his finger wrapped around the trigger. In one swift jump, he pushed himself up with his knees and hands. He swung the gun around toward the sound.

Nothing. No person. Nothing on the floor. The door was closed, and it looked like it was still bolted, as best as he could see in the dim moonlight that streamed through the window.

He put both hands down and pushed himself off the bed. The door slammed. He jerked around and the door was still closed. Cool air blew into his face, and the curtain over either side of the window rippled in the breeze.

With the gun still in his hand, he went to the door. The bolt was still locked.

He sat down on the bed and laid the gun beside him. He put his head in both hands and his elbows on his knees. *I've lost my mind. It's this crazy house. It's hainted. It has to be.*

Hours passed before he could sleep. When he did, he dreamed of a grave, full of snakes. He woke up and the bed was wet with sweat. *Tomorrow I need to find a mouse ear plant and make a tea.* It would make him puke and then he should not dream of snakes again. His Cherokee grandma on his Mama's side had told him that before she died.

He laid awake until he could see the shapes of the trees in the early morning light.

Chapter 16

Nathe took the dipper from the wall and pushed it down into the bucket of water. He poured the dipper full over his head. The water was warm from sitting in the sun, but it still felt good to feel the dirt and sweat slide down his face. He didn't even mind that it soaked his shirt. A slight wind was stirring, and the hint of a breeze made his wet body and clothes feel cooler.

Addie came out of the house. Her face was red, and sweat beaded on her forehead. "Lordy, if it don't rain soon and cool things off, we're all going to burn to a crisp. The house is so hot I can't stand it, but dinner is ready. Thank God, I cooked it all this morning before it got this hot."

Nathe nodded. "If it don't rain soon, we ain't gonna have much crop to harvest. If you and the children hadn't toted water from the creek and watered the garden, it would've already burnt up. I think somebody ain't paying the preacher.

Otherwise, we'd had rain by now. That ought to be a sermon for Sunday's meeting."

"Speaking of Sunday's meeting, there's going to be dinner on the ground. There is a picture taking man coming, and he will make pictures of any members that wants them. He was over at Scott's Creek Church last Sunday, and just about everybody there got theirs taken, I hear tell. I want our whole family at Mount Pleasant Church. Can you send word for Lottie and her family and Davie and his to be there to be in the picture with us? I wish Asa was here instead of working in Asheville. When I get the photograph, I'll write his name on the front where he would've stood. So they'll know there was another child. "

"I don't want pictures taken of me. That's just foolishness."

Addie narrowed her eyes and pointed her finger at Nathe. "It ain't foolish. I think it's a wonderful thing. Just think about our children's great grandchildren looking at our picture. Seeing their grandma when she was young. How we were a family. Years and years from now they'll know what we looked like."

"Why would they care what we look like? We'll all be dead and turned to dust by then. We won't be on their mind at all."

Addie pushed the sweat-soaked curls from her face. "You just let Lottie and Davie know. And, yes, you're going to be in the picture. If nothing else, you'll do it just for me. If you die like you think you're going to, then I want a picture to remember you by."

"Do you think you'll need a picture to remember me?" A grin spread across Nathe's face. He reached out and pulled her to his side.

"You behave Nathe Watson."

He reached behind him and got a dipper of water without her knowing. With a swoop of his arm, he poured the water over her head and let it run down her face and over her dress.

"You devil. Why'd you do that?"

"To cool you off. You needed it."

She tried to be mad, but it just felt too good to be cool for a little bit. "Then you go right up to the spring and get some more water seeing how you wasted what Sugar got this morning."

They looked at each other, and both started to laugh. Nathe pulled her closer and planted a kiss on her lips. "I'll do that, Mrs. Watson. Just as soon as I kiss you again."

"Get out of here. I got too much work to do to be playing like this." Her eyes lit up, and she grinned. She reached out and cupped his face with her hands.

"If we're too busy to show our love, then we're too busy. Don't you think? I still love you Addie, even after all these years. You gave us some mighty fine children. They're good and upright. Hardworking. You're why they're that way. You taught 'em good."

She patted his jaw and dropped her hands. "It takes two people to raise good children. You're the best thing that ever happened to me. You were a good Papa to Davie and to Clare. There was never a difference between the children I had before and the ones we made together. A good Papa."

Nathe took Addie's hand. "I've had a good life. Don't regret a day of it. Some days were better than others, but all were good. When I die, the one fact that makes me happy is that I'll see Clare again. I'll give her a hug for you."

Addie dabbed at her eyes with the edge of her apron. "I don't believe you're going to die now. You seem better. You have more breath. That doctor could be wrong. Doctors don't know everything."

"I wish it was so. But either way, I'm ready to go or ready to stay. He let go of her hand. "I'd better get that water you wanted. You may want another dipper full on yore head before this day cools off."

"I'll have dinner on the table when you get back from the spring."

xxx

Addie and Nathe, Davie and Pearline, heavy with child, Cling and his wife Bessie, Mariah Grace and her husband Beauregard, Maggie, and Sugar. They sat spread out on the last two pews in the back of the church. The church was packed full today. What with dinner on the ground and pictures to be made, people came out of the woodwork to church. They made sure to hold room on the seat for Lottie and her family. She was late!

As they stood to sing the first song, the back door opened, and Lottie and the children slipped inside. Everyone turned to see. Lottie's face turned bright red.

The children ran to sit with Cling and his family, and Lottie slipped in beside her Mama.

"Sorry I'm late, Mama. I had trouble finding good clothes that fit the children. I wanted them to look fine for the pictures."

"I take it Owen didn't make it."

"No, he was really tired he said. Just wanted to sleep. He works so hard all week long. Sunday is the only day he has."

"So do the rest of us, baby girl. He don't work no harder than anyone here. We still make time for our maker. It's the right thing to do. But it's just as well that he ain't here." She whispered.

"What do you mean?"

Nathe leaned forward and looked at the two women and frowned. Addie waved at him to sit back, and then talked quieter. "He ain't much part of the family anyway. Never comes over. Keeps you away as much as he can."

Lottie's chest rose and fell in a deep sigh. "I'm sorry. Let's just have a good day today. Let's be a family again, even if its' just for a little while."

xxx

Addie and Mariah spread a table cloth on the ground and brought the food and set it out. Maggie and Lottie spread out four quilts to sit on. It looked like enough food to feed an army. Addie, Mariah, and Davie's wife fixed plates for their husbands, and Lottie started plates for the children. Sugar helped her. After the men and children were eating, the women fixed their plates and went to the quilt where the men sat.

The preacher stopped by where they were. "Sister Watson, you're third on the list for pictures. I'll get you when they're ready for you. They've just started with the first group."

"Thank ye. We'll be ready."

The children were finished eating and getting up to play. "Sit down, youngins. I don't want you getting all dirty and sweaty before the pictures. Sit there until we get done." Addie told Lottie and Cling's wife, "Fix their hair. I brought some ribbons for the girls. They're in my crochet bag under the wagon seat. Fix them up real nice."

Nathe looked around. "I don't want to do this. There's no reason for those people that are yet to be born to see us like we are now. It's like freezing people in time. Like they didn't get older. But, we all do."

Lottie tied a hair bow on Annie May. "Papa, we'll never be like this again. Something might happen to one of us. For shore, we'll all be older."

"It might show what we look like in 1898, but it don't show what we've been through. That's what makes a person, not what they look like." Nathe looked at Addie.

Addie was mad. "You'll stand right up there with me and the children and be still like they tell us. Do you hear me? I think it would be nice if maybe someday Brody or Annie May could show their grandma and grandpa to their children and grandchildren. It would be like we were still alive and part of them."

"This ain't what the good Lord meant to happen. We are meant to die and new people come after us and take our place. We should be content to not show ourselves to a time and place that we're not welcome. They won't care nothing about us. They'll be living their own lives."

"Hush! Stop it right now, and let's go. They're ready for us. Just hold that mean look you have on you now. That way you'll look natural, and it'll be easy for you to stand that way as long as you need to for the picture!"

The children laughed. It was the way it had always been. Their Mama knew how to make the family come together and do what she wanted.

Chapter 17

Owen wiped the sweat on his forehead with the sleeve of his shirt. At the same time, he took the dipper from the nail on the wall and reached into the bucket, only to hear a tinkling metal sound. No water. He threw the dipper across the porch, and it hit the door with a clang and fell onto the floor. He yelled, "Lottie, get out here now. There's no water in the bucket, and I don't smell no food cooking. What's wrong with you?"

He turned and saw Lottie standing by the door. She had August by the hand, and Annie May and Brody were behind her.

"Annie May and Brody brought dinner home to me in this tub. Mama cooked it for me." She grabbed the tub and laid it on the porch. She pulled back the blanket that kept it hot. "Brody, take that bucket from yore Papa and run to the spring. Get it half full of water. That'll give yore Papa a drink, but it won't be so full that you can't carry it. I'll put supper on the table."

Owen kicked the tub. Lottie stepped up and, instead of it falling off the porch, it hit her in the stomach.

Owen screamed at Lottie, "You go get the water. A half bucket is not enough. I might want more than that. It's the least you can do for a man that works like a dog all day long trying to make a living for his family."

Brody picked up the bucket. Owen reached down and grabbed it from him. "I told yore Mama to go and get the water." He handed the bucket to Lottie.

She reached to take it, but Owen didn't let go. He stepped off the porch and put his face close to hers. "You went to yore Mama's again. I told you that you need to stay here and tend to our house. Quit traipsing off to their house every time I'm gone."

"Papa was sick today. Mama sent Sugar over to tell me to come to their house, so she could tend to us both. I've felt pretty poorly the whole time with this baby. She knew that I'm terribly sick and wanted me to come. She needed to make sure I'm eating good."

Owen sneered. "You'd be eating fine, if you'd cook once in a while. I'm sick and tired of half cooked vegetables because you're too sick to start cooking on time. If you don't eat good, it's yore own fault."

Lottie tried again to pull the bucket from his hands, but he held tight. She pulled harder. This time, he let it slip from his hands. She stumbled backward and fell. Owen laughed.

xxx

Lottie lay still, hoping the sick feeling would go away before she had to get up and fix Owen breakfast. The thought of smelling food made her feel worse. If she lay very still on the bed, maybe Owen would sleep a little longer.

Owen groaned and threw his arms above his head. "I know you're awake over there. Why aren't you already up cooking? I'm warning you right now that Glee wants me there before sun-up all next week. That means you must rise earlier than this every day."

"I don't think I can cook. I'm so sick. The thought of food makes me gag."

"I'm not asking you to cook. I'm *telling* you to get up, and fix my breakfast. A good wife would want to cook for her hard working man."

Lottie put her hand over her mouth to hold back the bitter taste that slid from her throat into her mouth. "I want to cook for you. I just can't. Please don't make me. I'm so very sick." She swallowed the hot, nasty water.

Lottie sat up and twisted her feet to the side of the bed. Owen took his feet and pushed them against Lottie's back. The push threw her against the wall. Her face slid down the rough lumber, and a burning pain shot through her face. She landed on her knees. She reached and touched the area where the pain ran down her nose and across her left cheek. Blood covered her hand. She felt it run onto her upper lip and into her mouth. Her eyes filled with tears. She jerked up the tail of her gown, and held it over her nose.

"Get in there, and start cooking." Owen jumped up and grabbed his pants and put them on. He sat back down on the bed and put on his boots.

Between gags, Lottie built a fire in the cookstove. She got on her knees and blew at the tiny flame. She needed to get a full blown fire as quick as possible so she could cook and then go back to bed. She crawled from the fire to a chair to steady her as she rose from the floor. Her hand reached out and landed on Owen's shoe.

"Get off the floor, you lazy thing."

"Arrgggggggggggggggg." She vomited on the toes of his boot and into the top of it. The green liquid covered the floor around his feet.

He kicked her in the face.

She fell hard on her back and rolled onto her stomach. Blood splattered across the floor from her nose that was bleeding again. Her lips felt thick and hurt where the toe of his boot had caught her mouth.

"I just lost my appetite." Owen left.

xxx

Beck tied his horse to the tree by the barn and walked to the back door. He saw Lottie leaning over a pan of water on the table, washing her face. He knocked lightly and, when she didn't look his way, he knocked harder. She turned, and he saw her bloody, bruised face. He didn't wait to be asked inside. She grabbed her stomach, and Beck caught her as everything went black.

When she came to, she was lying on her bed, and Beck was standing over her.

"Did Owen do this?"

She nodded and swallowed the lump in her throat. Her voice was a whisper. She grabbed her belly with both hands. "I don't know if the baby is alive or not."

Beck's gaze left her face and wandered down to the bulge under her dress.

She cried, "Oh, I just felt it. It's alive. Don't know if it's alright or not. Won't know that until he's born I suppose."

"A man is not much of a man, if he hits a woman. He is not worth the salt in his bread." Beck grabbed the hat he had forgotten to remove when he came in the house, jerked it off, and pulled it against his chest. "He ought not be hitting you. In fact, I think I could kill a man that would hurt a woman. Even easier, if I knew she was in the family way."

Lottie smiled sadly. She closed her eyes and tears slipped out the corners and ran into her ears. "You sound like Sugar. She said she could kill him without any shame. She'd just shoot him and tell God he died." She opened her eyes and looked at Beck.

They both took deep breaths and started to laugh. Softly at first, and then hard, until both were out of breath.

"I'm sorry, Miss Lottie. I know it's not a laughing matter, but I can see Sugar saying that. She don't have much patience with man nor beast. That's pretty apparent."

"It is. I worry about her. She's seen so much misery in my life, I'm not sure she'll ever marry. She hates men right now."

Beck fiddled with his hat, pulling it in circles, hand over fist, around and around. He chose his next words with care.

"Miss Lottie, like Sugar, I'm not sure I can contain myself if he hurts you again. I know it's asking a lot, but I want to take you away from this. I have family over in Tennessee, and they would help get a house for me, you, and the children. Nobody would have to know where we are. We'd just slip away and be gone"

Lottie shook her head. "No. Beck, I can't let you get in the middle of mine and Owen's problems. I've seen people get killed for a whole lot less. If there's anything you don't do in these mountains, it's get between a man and his woman. Wives are just like property. They treat it in the same manner as stealing. You know the opinion about thieves by the men here. They don't take kindly to them. I don't want you to get hurt."

"I ain't afeared of him. He's a coward. Only a coward would hit a woman. To save you and the children grief, and maybe even being killed, I think it's best if I get you out of here and not tell anyone where we're going."

Lottie bit her lip and looked around. "I sent the children to play outside. I didn't want them to see me until I clean myself up. All the noise woke them up this morning, but it was over and done with before they saw the worst of it. I need to get them back in here and let them eat."

Beck waved his hand. "I ain't saying we should leave this minute. It'll take a plan, and I'll have to think about how we can do it. If you have any ideas, let me know. Until then, we won't say a word to anyone else. I mean not one person. Do you understand?"

She nodded and tried to get up. "You lay right there for a bit. I noticed some tomatoes and a few cucumbers on the vines as I came by that burnt up garden of yores. I'll cut up some tomatoes and cucumbers and feed the children. They'll be fine for a couple of hours until you feel like fixing a bite for them to eat. I'll be back in a day or two and, by then, I should have a plan."

Chapter 18

The day started with fog, which rose from the creeks and moved into the lower parts between the mountains. Not a hint of the storm to come.

Addie and Maggie carried water from the spring and poured it into the black washpot that was already hot from the fire kindled underneath it. As they carried their last bucket to the house, they saw Dicey Mills coming up the road. She was their closest neighbor, but it was a good two miles by the road to her place. More than neighbors, Addie and Dicey were good friends.

"Hello Dicey. What are you doing out this fine morning? You're all dressed up like you're going to Sunday Meeting. The wind has cooled things off a bit."

Dicey listened to the small talk and then looked around at the sky. "There were owls hooting on the east side of the mountain last night. You know that means bad weather, don't ye? It feels like this wind is coming off rain to me. We're in for a storm today. I don't like it when it's real hot and then you start feeling cold air in between puffs of hot. Fierce storms come from days like that."

Addie smiled. "We could sure use the rain though. Our crops are almost burnt up. The horses and the men come in from plowing with dust so thick on them, they look like haints"

Dicey wrinkled her forehead and looked at the sky over the mountains to the west. "I should've known better than strike out for town like I did this morning. I'd planned on going to the post office to see if I had a package. With the wind getting up and that thunder over the mountains, I knew I needed to come back home. Guess I should hurry home and take cover during the storm. The children are up there all alone."

"I ain't heard no thunder."

Dicey wrung her hands. "It's there though. I heard just the low rumble of it, even though we don't see many clouds yet."

Addie knew her friend knew the weather like nobody else on Mills Ridge and most likely better than anyone in Jackson County.

"How are the children doing?" Addie loved the children like they were her own; a boy ten, a girl eight, and another girl five years old. Dicey was a widow.

"They're fine, but they'll be scared if they're alone when the storm gets here. I'll talk to you at church Sunday. Tell the family hello for me."

"I will. You be careful. Now, I hear the thunder. The storm is coming up fast. I'm not sure you'll make it before it hits."

Dicey pulled up her dress tail and ran down the road toward home.

Addie yelled to Maggie. "Get that fire stoked. Maybe we'll have time to finish the washing before the rain puts out the fire." She went into the house in search of lye soap.

Ten minutes later, there were loud rumbles of thunder that echoed over the mountains to the west.

Addie pulled her apron up and covered her arms against the cooler air that blew off the storm. She pulled it tight around herself and stepped onto the unpainted wooden floor. She stood beside Maggie, who was wringing her hands.

"Dicey was right. There was a storm a-brewing. I feel the change in the air, and the clouds are moving closer. Put that fire out before it blows embers and sets the dry woods or the house on fire. Leave the clothes in the tub for now."

The sky grew darker. Addie stood on the porch and watched the sky. "Listen to that rolling thunder. It sounds strange. The growl never ends. It's continuous rumbling. Do you hear that roar in the distance?"

The words had no more been spoken than the wind began to blow hard, and the trees whipped back and forth, breaking the stillness. On the mountain high above them, there was a loud crash. A large tree fell to the ground on the bank across the road from the house, taking several smaller

ones in its path. The winds were blustery at the
house, but seemed more violent on the mountain.
The fog had blown away, and large drops of rain
blew onto the porch.

"Quick Child, come in the house. The bottom
is going to fall out."

The porch began to tremble from the winds.
Maggie ran into the house and slammed the door.

Addie ran after her and found her trembling
and crouched behind the bed, scared to death.

"Just stay there near the bed until it's over. I
used to be scared of storms, too. You'll grow out
of it."

Maggie started to cry. "I'm twenty-two. If I
was going to grow out of it, don't you think I
would've by now? Are we going to die?"

"I don't believe we're going to perish. The
storm will pass just like all the others. We've lived
through lots of storms. We just have to believe the
good Lord will take care of us. "

Addie went back out on the porch to watch for
Nathe to come in from the fields, where he'd gone
to tell Beck his jobs to do that day.

xxx

The wind blew hard, and Nathe watched the
dark clouds roll upward from behind the western
mountains. The skies had darkened for an hour
each morning the last two days, but this time it
seemed like the clouds might actually hold rain.

Lightning flashed and, almost as quick, there
was a clap of thunder that shook the ground. The

storm was close, probably no further than the Indian reservation across the mountain.

Nathe grabbed one horse. Beck grabbed the other, and both ran toward the barn. They pulled them into a stable. A gust of wind blew the big outer door open and against the side of the barn. It took both of them to shut it. They ran toward the house as large drops of rain slapped them in the face.

Nathe stopped in the middle of the yard and raised both arms to the heavens. "Thank you God for rain." He looked at Beck who had stopped and was watching him. "I'm just so thankful. I guess somebody paid the preacher." He laughed.

Another jarring thunder set them on the run again, fighting against the whipping wind.

Addie stood on the porch and watched the clouds swirl and spin. A dark funnel formed just at the top of the mountain to the west. There were loud popping sounds that sounded like falling trees.

Nathe yelled to Addie above the sound of the wind, "Papa always said to open the back door and leave the front open. Do it quick."

Addie ran to the back of the house.

"Where's Sugar and Maggie?"

Addie yelled to be heard above the flapping curtains and falling limbs. "Sugar is at Lottie's house helping her with the canning. Maggie is hunkered down in the corner by the bed scared out of her wits."

Beck yelled, "I hope they ain't getting this storm over at Lottie's."

The men ran to another corner of the room and huddled away from windows and doors. Addie went to Maggie. The house shook under the force of the winds. A large limb slapped against the glass. Addie grabbed Maggie's face and pushed it against her chest. With one swing, she pushed her to the floor and covered Maggie's body with her own. There was a crash, and glass scattered across the floor. It was in their hair and on the furniture. Blood ran down Addie's neck from a scrape where she had been struck by a jagged chunk of glass.

Just as suddenly as the storm had started, it stopped. The heavy rain fell in sheets.

Nathe and Beck went outside to survey the damage.

Across the floor of the porch lay chips of wood from the fallen trees and limbs. There was something caught in the jagged glass against the grids of the windowpanes. Addie grabbed a coat hanging from a nail near the door and ran to cover the window to stop the driving rain. She stopped when she noticed a large piece of cotton material trapped in the glass fragments. Her face went pale and her breath caught in her throat. She pulled the fabric through the wooden frame of the window and untwisted it. She held a piece of the only dress she had ever seen Dicey Mills wear. She wore it every Sunday to church and had the same clothing on this morning when she passed their house.

"Oh merciful God! I wonder where Dicey Mills could be if her dress is here?"

xxx

Nathe and Beck looked at the strip of destruction the storm had plowed across the mountain and into the valley below. Thankfully, the house was in one piece, and so was the barn. There were trees lying on the ground on the mountain above them and across the road in both directions.

"I am on conscription to work this road all the way up to the Mills place and down to the Waynesville road. I guess the crops will have to wait. We'll need to make them passable. We'll go and see if the corn and tobacco took a beating after we look around here. Then, we'll check on the houses in the path of the storm. We need to make sure no one was hurt. We'll come back by the house and get a saw. First, we'll get the trees out of the road. We can cut them up later. If there are any logs big enough that are not broken to pieces from the fall, we'll take them down to the railroad and sell them to the lumber buyers from Asheville."

They heard Addie's scream, and both broke into a run toward the house.

"What's wrong? Why are you screaming? Is everyone all right?"

Addie held a piece of material in her hands, and tears ran down her face.

Nathe ran to her side. "What's that? Where did you get it?"

"It's material from Dicey Mills' dress she had on this morning?"

"You saw Dicey this morning? And she had that dress on?" He also remembered the material was the one dress she wore every Sunday. "Where was the material when you found it?"

Addie turned to the window and looked at the broken glass. Another piece of the material was still there from where she had torn it away from the bits of glass.

"Oh God, help us all." Nathe turned and looked at Beck. "Get down the mountain. Stop at every house between here and the main road and see if they've fared well. If they did, tell them to come up here and help us look for Dicey. Tell them what we found."

"Yes sir. I'll hurry." Beck put the bit in the horse's mouth, but didn't take time to put on a saddle. Instead, he rode it bareback and left with the horse in a run, weaving in and out around fallen trees.

xxx

Everyone else had damage to either their house or crops, but no lives were lost. Within the hour, four men and two women were at Nathe and Addie's house ready to join the hunt.

"Nathe left for Dicey's house as soon as you left, but I haven't heard from him. He told me to stay here until you all came and show you this piece of material. The rest may be on her body, and you might want to look for that. Now that you're going into the woods to find her, I'm going up to the house. If the children are alive, they'll be scared to death. They'll need some comfort."

Addie met Nathe on the path to the Mills house. He had the five year old girl on his shoulders and the other two by the hand.

Before she could speak, Nathe shook his head hard from side to side, and pushed his lips together tightly. It was plain he didn't want her to ask about Dicey.

"Let me have these sweet babies. I'll take them to the house with me. You can check on other things."

He nodded and pulled the five year-old off his shoulders. "Send all the men up to me, all but Beck. I'll send him to check on Lottie."

"I'll do that." She smiled at the children and shooed them in front of her. "Be careful making yore way to the road. I'm right behind you."

She looked at Nathe. He moved his lips in silence. "She's dead. Up in the trees behind the house. She didn't make it inside the house."

Addie swallowed the scream that tried to wrestle its way out of her throat. She turned and rushed toward the children. Nathe watched her. She would stop and rock back and forth from her waist, then stand up tall and run to catch back up with the children.

xxx

Addie made sure Dicey's children were in a place they could not see the outside. She had them laying on the bed.

A wife of one of the men helping Nathe stood in the door and raised her eyebrows at the children on the bed behind Addie.

"They cried themselves to sleep." Addie looked out the window and saw two men were carrying Dicey's body tied to a board. They took her to the barn.

The woman walked over to where Addie sat. "The men are going to work on a coffin. I'm going to tell the others. The house is torn up. I don't know how the children lived. Nathe said Dicey's body was wrapped around some limbs in a tree about a hundred feet behind the house. The children were wandering in the front yard yelling for their Mama. Nathe said for you to prepare to lay her out here at yore house until the burying."

Addie nodded in agreement. "The oldest told me her Mama laid down on top of them. The wind blew them up in the air then, they couldn't find her. Poor babies. Whatever will happen to them? She don't have no family that I know anything about. All are dead. We all need to put our thinking cap on and figure out who can take them."

"Yes ma'am. I'm going now to tell the others below. Nathe said to tell you that he looked off the overlook, and the path of the storm didn't go anywhere near any of yore children's homes, as best he could tell. So, you're not to worry about them."

Addie laid her hand on the woman's arm. "Thank you. I figured it didn't with the direction it seemed to be going, but it's good to hear from someone else that the family is fine. Still, after I prepare the house, I'll leave Maggie here to welcome the mourners, and I'll check on them anyway. It's what a Mama does." She looked over at Maggie. "That is if I can pry her off that seat she's sitting in. She's still shaking from the storm. She's afeared of storms like no one I've ever seen. Hope she gets over that."

xxx

Beck was glad that Nathe had sent him to check on Lottie. He needed to make sure that she and the children were all right.

Sugar was the first one to see Beck at the back door.

"Beck, what is wrong? Is it Papa?"

Lottie came running to the door.

Beck took off his hat when he saw her. "Yore Papa is fine. I just wanted to make sure that you all are doing well after the storm." He looked at Lottie and twisted his hat. "I mean, yore Mama and Papa wanted to know you were all right."

"Was the storm that bad over there? We just got a good, soaking rain here."

"The storm was mighty bad on the mountain." He told them about Dicey and all that had happened that morning.

"My goodness. I didn't think about it being that bad anywhere. I wonder if there were storms up at Glee's where Owen is working?"

Beck shoved his hat back on top of his head. "I'm sure Owen is fine. It didn't seem to be heading in that direction. I guess you'll know if he don't come home tonight. Well then, maybe you won't. Ain't there nights he don't come home, especially on payday?" He narrowed his eyes and stared at Lottie.

"Beckley Radford." Sugar's eyes were opened wide in shock.

"Never mind. I see you all are just fine. Yore Mama might come by too. You can tell her that I came like Nathe wanted me to do." With that, Beck left.

Sugar looked at Lottie and bent her head to the side and tapped her toe as she stared.

"Don't look at me like that. I have no idea what got into his head that he needed to check on us. Maybe it was you he was checking on. I don't believe a word of what he said about Papa sending him over here."

Sugar gasped. "I believe Papa sent him, but only because he seems to have this thing for you. I know he wasn't checking on me. When he first got here, he kept looking over my shoulder trying to see if you were still alive. He couldn't have cared less about me. Do you need to talk to me? Maybe tell me something?"

"I have nothing to talk about. He was just being kind and a good neighbor, making sure his boss's family was alive. Or else doing what Papa said."

Sugar grabbed her things. "I'm going home to check on things. You might not want to mention to Owen what Beck just did. You might have two black eyes instead of that knot on yore head I've stared at all morning."

Lottie touched the lump and grimaced. "I bumped it on a tree limb."

"You're a liar. Maggie and I both are amazed at how easy you lie for him. You're the sister that never would lie to anyone. Owen has changed you. I worry the day will come when someone will come to our door and say you're dead, not from a storm, but at the hands of that hateful man of yores. If things don't change, it may very well happen, you know. And if you let this carrying on with Beck get out, you'll both be dead."

Lottie turned red. "We're *not* carrying on. He's never been anything but kind to me. He's a true gentleman. He worries about me just like you do. That's all. He doesn't care for me in the way you're saying."

"Even if he doesn't, he can still get himself killed. No judge would think it strange if Owen did it. This is an awful thing. I never knew a man could be so mean until I knew Owen Thompson. He's not a man. He's the devil himself."

She rushed out the door. Her first step off the porch landed her in front of Owen.

"What's all this carrying on about?" Owen asked.

"There's been a death from the storm up above our house. I have to get home." Sugar looked back at Lottie and raised her eyebrows.

Owen turned to Lottie standing in the door. "Don't just stand there, get my supper. I'm tired and hungry. You're in yore seventh month, so don't be using that thing about being sick to me. I know from the other babies, you should be over with the sick spells long before now."

Chapter 19

Addie watched the mourners come to the coffin and cry over Dicey. It was not like they knew her all that well. Of course, they all saw her at church, but Addie didn't remember a single one of them ever coming by her house to visit. She would have known, because they had to pass her house to get to Dicey's.

At church, Dicey always sat in the back corner with her three children. The only time she ever missed service was when it rained hard or snowed. She stayed home, but only then because she was afeared to get her children out in bad weather. A little cold scared her to death. She'd come running to Addie to see if she thought she should get a doctor. Those two together examining a sick child *always* meant somebody needed to fetch the doctor, especially if it's a chest cold or the trots.

Dicey's husband had died of pneumonia, and Addie had lost a baby to the trots. Those deaths left them with a fear that never went away.

Addie had been the only true friend that Dicey ever had, so it felt right that she was the one that planned her wake. Addie, the granny doctor, had made poultices for Dicey's children's chest colds, stopped blood from their nosebleeds and deep cuts, took off warts from the children's hands, and blew out fire from their burns. Once, Addie chewed a wad of tobacco so she could put the spit from it on a wasp sting on her friend's hand. Afterwards, she had vomited from the horrible taste of the tobacco.

It could've been out of respect for Dicey, or because they were curious about the children, but Lottie didn't remember this many people at a wake in her life. They came and stayed, not came and went like usual. They brought food and paid their respects to the closed coffin. Afterwards, they showed their pity to the three children that Addie had dressed up and sat by the coffin to receive visitors. There was ten-year-old Elbert, eight-year-old Etta, and five-year old Essie. After a couple of hours of visiting, Addie had taken the children by the hand, brought them to Mariah and Beau and told them, "Take these babies to yore house. They don't need no more of this wake. They need somebody to love them and feed them, not out of pity but pure love. I think you two are the ones that should do that. You ain't got no babies of yore own. These could be yore children. Dicey would have liked it to be that way."

Mariah smiled and gathered them to the side of the wagon. As Beau picked them up and put them in the back, Mariah ran back into the house to get the dish in which she had brought food. A woman grabbed her arm as she came out of the house. "I'd be interested in farming out that oldest girl you're taking away. She looks strong, and I could use her around the house for planting and gardening. She could earn her keep. I hear tell that the boy might be wanted by the Johnson's. Their oldest son ran away, and they need help in the fields. That little one will be the hardest for you to get rid of."

Mariah felt sick. "They're not available for farming out, and I don't plan on getting rid of any one of them. They're not horses or mules on the auction block. They're little children, and they need a home, not a job. They need a momma and a papa, not a taskmaster. They're a family that needs a home. They're brother and sisters and shouldn't be separated."

"Hmp. Then good luck finding a home that'll take all three. You should be glad any of us are willing to take even one in. In no time, you'll be putting them on the train to the orphanage in Asheville. They'll separate them. At least here, they might all be in the same county and could see each other."

Mariah grabbed up her dress tail and ran down the steps. She jumped in the wagon beside Beau. "Let's get our children and get out of this place. If you don't hurry, I may well hit that woman. These people are savages."

Beau reached over and took her hand. "Let's show them their new home. Our children. I like the sound of that."

In the house, Addie had taken the children's place by the coffin, and sat there all night. The others would nod at her as they stood by the casket, then head to the kitchen, fix a plate, and carry it outside in the yard to gossip and visit.

Much later, when she was by herself with Dicey's body, she looked at the casket and remembered many years ago as she has sat by another, smaller one. A baby girl wrapped in a quilt. She knew now, as she knew then, this was walking the last mile you could with a person.

xxx

It was late the next day before they carried the body by wagon to the church and had a funeral.

Lottie and Owen came in as the preacher stood up and came to the pulpit. Owen had her by the elbow and pushed her to the back seat. He took the seat next to her on the aisle. Lottie had on a dark bonnet with the brim pulled down low on her forehead.

Halfway back in the congregation, Sugar left the seat where she was sitting. She pushed against Owen's knee as she tried to get by him and sit by Lottie. He let her get both legs even with his knees, and then slammed her legs against the pew in front of him. Pain went through Sugar so sharp that she felt sick. She looked at him with tear-filled eyes from the throbbing in her leg. She took a step and pushed her foot down and shifted all her weight onto his foot. He grunted loud enough that several people looked back at them. He shoved

Sugar off his foot, and she fell into the seat on the other side of Lottie.

Lottie never looked up during the commotion, but kept her eyes on the floor. She bent her head enough to make the shadows on her face darker. Sugar took her arm and laid it behind Lottie on the back of the seat. She waited a moment, then reached up and grabbed the back of the bonnet and gave a jerk. The bonnet fell on Lottie's back.

Lottie jerked around and faced Sugar. Tears ran down her face. Both eyes were blotchy red with a touch of black settling below each eye.

Sugar's hands curled into fists. She pushed them against her legs.

Lottie looked at the fist between her and Sugar. She reached down and covered it with her right hand. With her left hand, she reached back and pulled the bonnet back over her head and jerked at each side until it again shadowed her face. Her right hand was trying to pry Sugar's fingers out of making a fist.

Sugar jerked her hand away from Lottie. "I'll kill him," she whispered against the side of the bonnet near Lottie's ear.

"Shut up. You won't do nothing. There is nothing you can do." She whispered back.

The commotion got the attention of Beck, where he sat across the aisle and up two pews in front of them. It was a perfect angle to see the blackened eyes when the bonnet came off. He jumped up and went toward the door. His face was red and his lips pulled tight together. He looked first at Lottie and then at Owen. Sugar saw Owen laugh and fake a spit toward the angry Beck as he passed by.

The singing was like the usual singing at church. The leader said "Amazing Grace how sweet the sound," and the rest of them sang it together, and in the same manner right on through the entire song…the leader speaking a few words and then the others sang. Several women sat on the front row beside Addie, and they moaned and cried with her at each break in the song. There were four songs, and then the preacher preached his sermon.

They laid Dicey in the damp earth in the church cemetery. Addie had made bouquets of wild flowers and given them to each child. They dropped them onto the coffin after they lowered it into the hole. Again, Mariah and Beau took them away…before they covered her up and before the others got a chance to pinch their cheeks and tell them how pitiful they were to lose both father and mother. They did not want to hear another person discuss who was to get what child, or tell about all the hard work they would have to do to earn their keep.

The rest of the people used the time for visiting. They walked around to join groups and talk in reverent, quiet voices.

Sugar managed to pull Lottie away from Owen long enough to ask her what happened.

"What do you think happened? It was just like always. No matter what I do, it's never the right thing."

Sugar watched Owen as she talked. He glanced their way once and laughed. "One thing is different this time. You admitted he hit you. For once you didn't give an excuse or take up for him.

If Papa sees this, he's a dead man. I'd kill him, but you'd probably never speak to me again. I hate that sorry excuse for a man. I don't know what God was thinking when he made him."

"Don't worry about this, little sister. It won't last much longer."

Sugar forgot all the bawling out she had planned to do to Lottie when she heard that. "What are you going to do? If you'll tie him to the bed the next time he comes in drinking, I'll beat him to death. We'll hide his body so deep in the mountains, nobody will ever find him."

Lottie couldn't help but smile. "Nothing like that. I just think I'll take a friend up on his offer to get me and the children away from here. Let him take me so far away that Owen can't find me."

"I'm not sure there is a place that far away. He'll hunt you down. Killing him is a better way to go." Sugar reached out and wiped the tear away from below her sister's eye, which was getting blacker by the hour.

Lottie jerked from the burning pain of the tears. "Even if he finds me, I won't come back. He'll just have to accept that. I'll never come back as long as he's here and alive."

It was all too plain for Sugar. "Oh Lottie. I'll miss you so bad. You need to go, but what will I do without you? You'll tell me where you are, won't you? I'll never tell another soul."

"I'll have to tell Papa and Mama. And you too, of course. I know none of you will tell him. It has to be far away from here."

"Is it Beck? Is he the one that offered to take you away from here?"

Lottie nodded. "He's a kind man. He's never laid a finger on me for any reason. I trust him. He'll do what is right by me. His family will take me and the children in, he said. Shhhh. Here comes Owen. We'll talk about it later."

Sugar stared at Owen with all the hate she could muster until he walked up and stood right in front of her. Then she spat on him. He pulled his arm back ready to hit her but stopped and looked around.

"What? You can't hit with a crowd around? You have to be somewhere nobody sees how low down you are when you do it."

Owen swallowed hard and clenched his fists. "I'll make you sorry…"

"This is not Lottie you're dealing with. I ain't afraid of you. You're a puny, good-fer-nothing excuse for a man. You're lower than a snake's belly and sorrier than an egg-sucking dog. If I was Lottie, I'd kill you and hide you in the mountains where nobody could ever find you."

He dropped his hands to his side and laughed, too loud for a funeral. The others looked around to see who would disrespect the dead with laughter.

Owen laughed at Sugar. "Don't worry. Yore time's a-coming. I hear that Chastain boy asked you to marry him. Said he's going to get the marriage license next week. He'll straighten you out real good. You'll learn to toe the line."

Lottie grabbed her arm and pulled her around. "Is that true? Are you going to marry Tolliver?"

"It's true he asked me. I haven't decided if'n I'll marry him or not. If all men are like this sorry thing you married, I'll never marry." Sugar jerked her arm loose from Lottie and turned back toward Owen. He was walking away. "Hey, Owen."

Owen turned around. "Yeah, what do you want?"

"You have to sleep, old man. Things can happen while a man is sleeping."

Owen took one step back toward them. "Are you threatening me?"

"What does it sound like to you? Just wanted you to know how dangerous it is to sleep when you're as mean as the devil when you're awake.   It might even be dangerous to eat. Food makes people real sick sometimes. They even die from it."

Owen's brow creased for a minute, then he laughed. "That works two ways, girl."

He left them as Lottie held the screaming Sugar.

Chapter 20

The men were in suits and looked at Glee in his dirty clothes. They wrinkled their nose and sniffed. The spokesman of the group said, "Mr. Hooper. I'm glad you could meet with us today."

"The load was to yore liking, I hope."

"Yores is the best we get, for sure, for the most part. So good in fact that we are here to inform you that we need you to give us two extra loads a week."

"That's not possible."

The men looked at each other. The older of the two reached into his pocket and took out a paper and handed it to Glee. "This states that unless we get those two extra loads, then we'll be forced to look elsewhere to someone that's more accommodating than yoreself. This is yore last chance. I take it you did not read the entire agreement."

Glee's face reddened. He tried to convince them. "I just hired another man a week ago. That will possibly help me have one extra load."

"We said two, but you meet us here next week with yore last load. We'll talk about yore success or lack thereof. We'll take smaller trees if you want. Clear cutting makes it go faster. Is that agreeable?"

Glee knew there was nothing to do but shake hands. He'd do his best to get the men to work harder. He'd work harder too. He didn't want to lose this contract. He was still short of making the money he needed to get away from Jackson County before Nathe knew what was going on.

xxx

They had worked extra hard all week, and they were still short of the required amount. He ordered the extra hand and Owen to be there before sunrise, and they worked till past dark. Maybe he should have taken the man's advice that day in the general store and made whiskey. Sure would have been easier than cutting logs. They had cut all day and loaded at night for two days. Everyone was tired with no more than three or four hours of sleep a night, but Glee felt it would be worth it in the end. He might hold the men's pay on the last load. Using their money could make it possible for him and his family to get to a train to Asheville and then on to Virginia. He wouldn't be as rich as he had hoped, but there should be enough to live well for a while.

"Why are you two just now getting here? We left three logs to load this morning because you were bellyaching last night about being tired. It'll be sunrise in an hour, and we'll not be ready to start cutting because you're late."

Owen growled, "You're working us too hard. I'm about sick of this. It's not worth this for the puny amount we're making."

Glee handed a rope to Owen. "Shut up and start pulling, or you won't get paid a cent for the week."

xxx

They tied the logs to the wagon, cut two more trees, and planned to get them loaded and off to meet Glee's men by nightfall. They were so tired, which made them careless. Neither of them paid any attention to the huge dead limb high in the tree as they cut below. There was a sound of a loud crack. Smaller bits of branches fell on their heads. They looked up to a large limb breaking smaller ones as it crashed down.

Owen and Glee dived away from the branches. When it hit the ground, they were caught in the upper, smaller limbs. It took only a few minutes to push them aside and get up.

Owen swiped at the blood from a cut on his arm. When he looked up, Glee was standing over the body that had been pinned under the heavy end of the limb. Owen rushed to his side. Up through his stomach was a stick that pushed into his back and out his belly. Blood ran from his mouth and his eyes were set in a far-away look.

Owen jerked on Glee's arm. "Let's get him up and see if we can get him to come to."

"He's dead, you idiot. What we need to do is to drag his body and throw it over the cliff down at Thunderhead Point."

Owen felt sick. Glee kept talking, "Nobody will ever miss him. He's a convict. He broke out of jail. We both just have to keep our mouth shut."

"But…" Owen tried to explain he wanted no part of it.

"You'll do as you're told. Now get a hold of him, and help me drag him down there. We need to get back to work."

"I can't believe you're not going to at least try to find his family. That's low."

"Shut up. You go and tell people if you want to, but you'll be in as much as trouble as me for cutting and selling lumber on somebody else's property."

"I only work for you. You're the one that's doing it."

"You think they'll believe that? And you married to the owner's daughter? Ha! You're crazier than I thought. I picked you because of how bad you hate Nathe Watson, even if you did marry his daughter. You knew what you were doing when you started. Don't pretend otherwise. Maybe I need to let the law in on some other things I know about you while I'm at it."

Owen jerked up the man's feet and yelled at Glee. "Get his arms, and let's get him down there."

xxx

"The goods are fine. Some of the best we ever got, although that last load seems a log or two short of the others."

Glee ran his hands through his sweaty hair. He had hoped they wouldn't notice. His help getting killed had held them back on yesterday's cutting. "I'll try to make that up on the next load. The road will be drier, and I can haul off a bigger load." Glee figured he would cut this last load a little lower on the mountain, and then get out of the county.

"Yore land is what I want to talk to you about. The Mountain Land and Mining Agency from Webster seems to be having a good deal of luck in finding us timber land to buy from their advertisement in the Tuckasegee Democrat. From the beginning, I wanted to purchase yore land and not just the logs. I'd still like to do that. I take it there's more where this came from."

Glee hemmed and hawed, not sure how to convince them they only needed the logs. "This here is family land. I might not be able to sell it right now."

"We have a number of people with money that would pay good for yore land. Just think. You can sell the land, and then we'll pay you to log it, too. Don't that sound like a good deal?"

Glee nodded his head. He wrinkled his forehead and attempted to swallow the lump in his throat. *I wonder if I could get the pay and get far enough away before they found me.* The lump went away.

The older gentleman said, "There's one tiny thing I need to clear up with you. I was privately informed that you might not be the owner of the land on which you are acquiring the timber. Is that true?"

Glee snorted and folded his arms around his ribs. "I took one of yore men up there and showed him that timber right before we made the deal. He saw my house when he was there. Of course, that land is mine."

"Well, if that be the case, why don't you just sell it to us? You'll make double the money, selling the land and making money doing the logging. We could probably make provision for you to stay in yore house for the entirety of yore life or deed off a section for you to have the house and some tillable land."

The men took advantage of Glee's silence and said. "Go on to yore house or back to logging, and we'll contact you again in a week. You think long and hard about it. You'll not get a better deal than I'm offering, I assure you."

They shook hands, and the men left for the train station.

Chapter 21

Davie was angry. If Papa knew what Glee and his men were doing, he would be mad enough to kill someone. Of course, Davie didn't know if it was true. He'd overheard only part of the conversation. Words like logs and money had caught his ear. But the clincher was when one said, "Glee better hope Nathe dies before he finds out what he's doing, or he'll kill him." They went on talking about the Hooper-Watson feud. One of the men wore a store-bought suit. The other man said that he had worked as a prisoner on the railroad near Balsam. After he had paid his dues for the crime, he told them he had gone to Glee to ask for work but was told that he had already hired two men.

XXX

The horse's sides were puffing in and out from the strain as Davie came to my old house. He left the horse there to rest and started out on foot toward the top of the mountain.

Davie had thought long and hard about the mountains and their responsibility to care for the land. So much of the timber had been cut from the mountains that there were no roots to hold the dirt together. The last rain had caused mud to slide down several mountains, cleaning the land clear down to the rocks underneath. Now it wouldn't grow timber or anything else. Two families that lived below one mountain had lost everything. Another family not only had their possessions destroyed, but two of their children had died in the mud slide. All because people were greedy, clear cutting timber and not just taking what was needed of the older trees.

Nathe would never want the tree cuts, much less clear cut, and that was what Glee had probably done.

He didn't know if he would find Glee at his house or in the woods, but Davie planned to hunt him until he was found.

Davie stopped to catch his breath at Thunderhead point. It was then that he heard the familiar sound of chop, chop, chop. It was the sound of two axes hitting, one right after the other. The sound came from a stand of trees off the main road that couldn't be seen, maybe not for years unless a person was hunting and came upon it.

A man yelled, and then there was a crash as a tree fell against others around it, taking branches and limbs with it until they all hit the ground.

Everything seemed quiet, and then Davie heard one yell, "Clean off the limbs and I'll be back soon." Two voices came closer. One sounded like a child.

Davie slipped behind the tree beside the flat rock near the edge of the mountain. He waited until they were beside him and stepped out. "What do you think you're doing, Glee? You don't own this land. You can't be cutting the timber."

"You don't own the land either. It's Nathe's. He knows I'm cutting."

"That's a lie, and you know it. He would've told me. We've been wondering how you were going to get money to pay for living here. Now, I know. You won't like what's going to happen once Nathe finds out."

Glee took off his hat and scratched his head. He patted his son on the head. "Sit down here, son. I need to talk to Davie. We'll be on our way in a bit." He came to where Davie stood. They walked out to the edge of the mountain at Thunderhead Point. Six buzzards glided below them in circles.

Glee reached out and took Davie's upper arm. "You, boy, are a Hooper just like I am. Why are you taking his side? I can give you a cut of this. It would be a just share for keeping quiet. Nathe thinks he's better than us, just because he owns a lot of land...his grandpa's place, Addie's place, and land over on Mills Ridge. He's rich. We're as deserving as him. Have you forgotten that he was going to kill my Papa when I was a little boy?"

Davie folded his arms and stared at Glee. "You must've forgotten that he could've done that and no one would've been the wiser, but he didn't. And where I live is now my farm. Papa gave it to me. I own it free and clear."

Glee spat at Davie's feet. "Yore Papa. He ain't yore Papa. Don't pretend to be a Watson. You're Hooper, clean to the bone. If you think you want to be a Watson, maybe I need to treat you like one." He swung a fist at Davie.

Davie stepped back and, as he did, Glee lost his footing and fell on the ground. When he tried to get up, the dirt between the rock and the edge slid away and Glee slid toward the side of the mountain.

Davie grabbed at Glee's arm just as his body went off the edge. His hand slid down Glee's arm to his hand, catching it at the wrist. With his other hand he grabbed at his shirt. Davie sat down. The weight of Glee pulled on him, and he slid down closer to the edge. He let go of the shirt and grabbed behind him for something to hold onto. He grabbed a young sapling that grew from the base of the decaying oak tree beside the large rock. It steadied him enough to hold on to Glee's wrist for the time being. Glee's jerk lessened as he got a toe-hold on something that steadied him, but his weight still pulled on Davie.

The young boy ran toward them and lay down on his belly to look over the side. Glee's face was red, and a pulse throbbed in his neck. A cord of muscle ran from the back of his jaw into the top of his shirt. He pulled at Davie's arm until it felt like it was separating at the shoulder. Glee stilled and looked at Davie and back to his son, pleading for him to send the boy away.

"Go get help. Hurry." The child turned and ran back in the direction he and his Papa had come.

"You're bigger and stronger than me. Get me back up."

"You think I should pull you back up? And why would I want to do that? You're stealing us blind. Papa's good to you, and you're as mean as a hornet. Taking what's not yorn. You're a thief, stealing from the very ones that have helped you."

"He's not yore family. I'm family. Remember, we're both Hoopers.   You should be helping me, not accusing me." Glee reached up with his other hand and grabbed Davie's sleeve.

"You're not hanging. You've got a toe hold. Help me get you back up."

"Don't let go. I may have a hold of this root, but I can't get up by myself. A Hooper would not let another one fall to his death."

"Quit saying that. I ain't a Hooper. I took Nathe's name and his part. He was good to me. None of you ever came to help my family when we were starving. You didn't help my Mama when my baby sister died. None of you even came to the funeral."

"I was just a little boy when that happened. Don't be blaming me. It was because you was living with a Watson."

"Where did you hear about that being the reason? Nobody knew he was a Watson then, not even us."

"Just get me back up there, and we'll talk this through. I'll even give you a cut on the money from the logs. This is land that Nathe will never walk over. He's a dying man. There's no way he'll know the trees are gone, unless you tell him. He don't need the money, and we do. You could use it, I know. Maybe build that woman of yores a nice house. Maybe a dollar on every ten would be fair."

Davie purposely let his grip slip a little. It showed that Glee's was not in a strain to keep from falling. "You are a useless piece of trash. The likes of you are what give the Hoopers a bad name. If Papa dies, you're stealing from *me*. He'll leave me this land."

It sounded like a root snapped, and Glee gave a harder pull on Davie's arm, but he was still not about to actually fall. "You act like the Watsons are without guilt. They've killed as many as we have and injured more."

"Papa told us. But Nathe didn't do nothing. Why hurt him?"

"I'll tell you. Just get me back up there, and we'll talk. My arm is getting too tired to hold on." Glee let go of Davie's with one arm but held on with the other. He clawed at roots that jutted out, but, one by one, they broke as he pulled on them.

Davie gave a hard pull, and Glee landed on his belly on the ground in front of him. "It's about time. You're a sorry…"

Davie narrowed his eyes. "Don't say too much. You're still on the edge and one good push would send you over."

Glee spat, and the spit landed on Davie's arm. Davie knew that if he didn't leave right now,

turning the other cheek would not happen. He
turned just as Glee swung a fist at him. Davie felt
the wind of the planned blow and turned back.
With nothing to connect to the punch, Glee lost his
balance again and fell. He slid again over the edge
and grabbed the same root, but this time it pulled
away from the dirt inch by inch. The root broke.
Glee's hand grabbed a sapling a little lower down,
holding tight to its frail trunk. He yelled, "This is
all yore fault. You're trying to kill me."

Davie stuck his foot through a root that was in
the ground on each end but made a curve above the
dirt. He got a good toe hold and hoped it would
hold his weight. He lay down on his belly and
reached over the side. "If I was trying to make you
die, you'd be gone right now. I'd just leave you
here."

Glee took his one hand loose from the sapling,
and reached up. His hand wouldn't reach Davie's.
"I can't reach you. You have to help me." Glee
opened his eyes wide, and tears ran down his
cheek. He kicked and pulled harder at the sapling.

"Don't struggle. That'll never hold you if you
keep jerking at it."

Glee grew still. "Don't let me die. Please
don't let me die. I have a family. Pull me back
up."

"I can't reach you this time. Can you get yore
foot on anything down there to push on?"

The limb shook as Glee kicked. "I can't feel
the side of the mountain with my lower body. I
think the dirt has washed away down there. Please,
please help me!" Davie had never seen that kind of
fear in a man's face. Gone were the mocking and
the arguing.

"I want to. I really do, but I can't reach you. You have to find a way to help yoreself."

"My arms are tired. I can't hold on much longer."

Davie got up and went to another angle, to see from another direction, what was below Glee.

"Don't leave me. I beg you. Don't go away."

"I'm not gone. I'm just trying to see what you might put yore foot against to help me pull you up."

Glee screamed. "God, help me. Please help me. Davie, come back. Davie. Davie."

Davie could hear him but didn't take the time to answer. He went back to the path. With one hand, he took a larger sapling than the one that Glee had hold on. With the other hand, he pulled out the small axe that hung on his side. With one quick hit, the limb broke free, and Davie brought it to where Glee hung.

"I'm right here. I have a limb that I think you can hold on to that might get you back up."

"Hurry. Please hurry."

Davie cut the leather string that held the axe to his side and used it to tie the limb to his arm. He threw the other end of the sapling over the side, and he heard Glee grunt as it hit him in the face. "It hit me. My face is bleeding."

Glee's son had gotten Owen. He yelled down to Glee. "What happened? The boy said I needed to come and help, said you was dying." Owen lay down and slid to the edge. He could hear Glee's screams.

Davie looked at Owen. "Thank God you're here. Help me get Glee back up. He fell."

Davie yelled, "Glee, get a good grip on the limb I dropped. Owen is here to help until we can get you far enough up to reach our hands."

"Owen, please help Davie. He can't do it by himself. I'm heavier than him. But you have to hurry, because I can't hold on much longer."

Owen eased out a little further to get a quick look at his friend's face. "What happened?"

"I fell. Shut up and get me back up there. Oh God, help me. My hands are slipping."

Davie shook the limb that was tied to his hand. "Do you have a good hold yet?"

"I've got it with one hand. I'm going to let go of the other and try to get a good hold with both hands."

"No! Wait. Pull on it, and make sure it feels strong enough to hold yore weight before you let go." Davie yelled.

It was too late. Davie's arm felt like it had been pulled away from his body as Glee's weight pulled on the limb tied to his arm. He screamed in pain. Suddenly, the limb no longer felt heavy. Glee's screams faded as he fell farther and farther toward the holler below.

Davie and Owen stared at each other.

Davie got off his stomach and sat down on the rock. He leaned over and put his head between his hands. "I tried to save him. How am I going to tell his wife that he's dead, much less what he was doing when he died?"

"Do you think he might be alive?" Owen ran to another perch that looked deeper into the holler. Davie had a burning taste in his mouth and spit the bitterness between his feet. "Not a chance. That falls four hundred feet straight down. The bottom has a pile of jagged rocks that have fallen in the past. All of them rocks are amidst a hell of tangled laurel of about twenty five acres. There's no way he could live, and there's not much way of getting to him. By the time we did, his body would be eaten by all these buzzards I see circling. It's like they knew something was going to happen."

"I would've thought you let him go on purpose, if I had not heard him with my own ears say he fell. What happened? The boy said you were fighting."

Davie narrowed his eyes at Owen. "We never fought a lick. We were talking, and Glee jerked around, lost his footing, and slid off."

Davie stood and rubbed his shoulder. The pain was horrible. "I guess we better go and tell somebody. I don't think we should try to find his body, even though I think everyone deserves a decent burial, if it's at all possible."

Owen peeked over the side one more time. "I'm not sure we'd find him if we tried. I need to get my supplies." In his mind, he thought about the two bodies that lay below.

"What work are you doing?" Davie wanted to see if Owen would admit his part in the thievery.

"Uh, I've got to get out of here."

"You might want to do that. I was coming to see Glee to tell him that word got out that he was stealing from Nathe. Wonder what Lottie will think when she finds out that you've been stealing from our Papa?"

Owen's face twisted with anger. "She thinks what I tell her to think. She's my wife." Owen turned and ran back to get his axe and crosscut saw.

xxx

Beck met Nathe at the foot of Rich Mountain. The horse Beck rode was hot and lathered from running.

"What are you doing here? I thought I sent you to Sylva to get a load of supplies. The train was supposed to be there at noon today." Nathe shaded his eyes with his hands and looked up. The sun stood about 11:00 in the morning. "I hope they find someone to leave the shipment with. Get on back up there, and get it."

"I'll go back as soon as I tell you what I came to tell you. I think you'll find it important." Beck alit off the horse and held the reins in his hands.

"Well, get on with it. Tell me what you have to say."

"Did you know that Glee has been cutting lumber off yore land and selling it to a lumber company from Asheville?"

Nathe's face reddened, and he took two long steps that brought him face to face with Beck. "He wouldn't do that. You must be wrong. How do you know? Who told you?"

"I heard it with my own two ears. Glee was talking to a man from the lumber Company. They were complaining that he wasn't getting trees to them fast enough, that they were going to cut him loose and not do business with him unless he started bringing in more logs. They said that a load every three days was nowhere near enough; that unless he got it to a load every two days, the deal was off. He told them that he would try to hire another man to help."

"Where is he getting logs? You must surely be wrong about it coming from my land. I would have heard about it."

Beck mounted his horse. "I don't rightly know the particulars, but I am sure that he is cutting on yore land. Up high in the mountains where no one hears the trees fall, and there's large timber. The railroad loves to make lumber from trees like that. I followed him around for a bit. He asked some men about their workers. He wanted to hire some of them, if they could spare them. Of course, they told him no. Most all the workers he was asking about were prisoners. He mentioned that, if they could spare even one of them, he would bring them back to check in every two days when he brought in a load. That didn't work with them. They told him the answer was the same as it had been the last time he came looking for workers. This was surely not the first time he had come to hire someone. He asked them to pass the word around that he was looking for a worker.

"The thing that made me know it was on yore land was when he told another man that inquired about the job that the trees were near his house. He told them he was clearing to make land to plant more crops and was selling the trees to make some extra money. He mentioned any workers could stay in a barn nearby while they worked so as to not have to go all the way back to his home. He said he had let another worker stay there earlier this month."

Nathe pulled at his lips and shook his head. "He must have let them stay in Amps' old barn. He has no right selling my lumber. Some Asheville lumber company has tried to get my trees for over two years. I'll not let them destroy our mountains. I see what happens when they cut the trees. The land just falls off the mountains in slides of mud at every heavy rain we get, right down to bare rock. Then, it won't grow nothing but spindly trees. Not a single crop can produce on it. I know they need lumber, but they ain't getting mine."

"I thought you ought to know. I'll get back to town and pick up that shipment. I left the wagon there and rode the horse here, so as to save time."

"You did the right thing. I'm sorry I yelled at you earlier." Nathe patted the horse on the neck. "The horse is cooled down, so you can ride back. Don't tell no one else what you heard or saw. I'll take care of this."

Beck reined the horse around and left.

Nathe was angry. Instead of going by Lottie's as he'd planned, he turned the horse toward Rich Mountain.

xxx

At the Tuckasegee River, Nathe stopped and let his horse get a drink and rest. He dropped the reins and squatted on a root that jutted out of the water.

"Where you headed?"

Nathe slipped at the sudden voice. His foot hit the water, and he fell back against a tree. "Amps, this is it, right? The Hoopers taking advantage of the Watsons again? It won't end until the last Hooper is in their grave."

"It could be the last Watson. Are you thinking that's what you should do? Kill a Hooper?"

The horse stepped away from the water and shook as though he was trying to shake the saddle off his back. Nathe grabbed his reins and led him to a patch of grass and let him graze. "That's right. I'm thinking it's time. I think there's not a man on this mountain that would find me guilty, if they knew what Glee has done. Not that we get much justice here."

"Why do you think he did it? Why did he sell the lumber?"

"I don't give a bear's paw about *why* he did it. I only care that he did. He stole from me. He's a thief and a liar. He said he was share cropping. He hasn't done much of nothing. All the time, he planned to steal from me. Do you think he'd have given me my part of the money? Of course not, not that I want him to. I want the trees. I want them in the ground, standing straight to the sky, growing strong and holding the dirt together and saving the mountain like I have always known this mountain to be. He don't have no rights to my mountain."

I sat down and motioned for Nathe to sit. "I don't want to sit down. I have something to take care of."

"I know I may not be able to talk you out of this. I do understand how you feel, but remember what you're teaching yore family."

Nathe and I locked eyes. His eyes didn't blink as he said, "We don't have a thing to worry about. I'm teaching them to protect what is theirs. You don't let a thief walk away. When I get through, there'll not be a Hooper left to feud with."

"You think this is only about Hoopers? It's not. It's about the way you try to settle arguments. You need to cool off that temper of yores first and foremost. Hoopers won't always live near Watsons. Names will change as yore girls marry, but there'll always be problems. If not a Hooper, it will be a Johnson, or a Smith, or maybe a Crawford. The names will change."

I felt there was nothing else that could be said to reason with him. "This is the last time you'll see me on this side of life. It was my last chance to try to make you see reason. I wanted you to learn something from the past and make yore family a better future. I've done all I can do. The way it all turns out is in yore hands, but you hold two sides of this coin. Yore eternal destiny and yore children's lives, for generations to come, are in yore hands. Make wise decisions, for they're yore decisions and yore's alone. It's bound up in yore own heart. The decision is made in yore mind and carried out with yore own hands. Good-bye."

This time, Nathe didn't miss my leaving. I faded into the fog before his eyes. I was gone into the air like a vapor, a dream, snow that melts in the heat of the day.

xxx

Davie was almost at the bottom of the mountain when he met Nathe.

"Davie, I'm glad you're here. Glee is stealing us blind. He's been cutting down trees off the land and selling them for his own profit."

Davie looked at Nathe's red face. "I heard. Beck told me when we saw each other on the road. He was coming to find you, and I was on my way into town. What are you planning to do?

Nathe stood up in the stirrups and put his hand on the gun in a sheath on the back of the saddle. "What needs to be done. A thief should not expect to live long. A Hooper thief especially. They have bad blood. It's in their nature. I'll stop this from ever happening again. Every Hooper will be in the ground before the day is done."

Davie swallowed hard and took a deep breath. "So do you plan on starting with me? I'm a Hooper."

Nathe's hips fell back into the saddle. "You're not a Hooper. You're a Watson."

"No Papa, by blood, I'm a Hooper. If it's bad blood that the Hoopers have, then it runs in me, too. Are you planning on doing it now, or do I watch my back until you make the decision to do it at some other time? Oh I forgot, it'll be before the day is done."

"I don't think of you as a Hooper. I think of you as my son, Davie Watson. You're as much mine as Cling, Asa, Mariah, Maggie, Lottie, or Sugar. You're all my children."

"I think of you as my Papa too, but we're not talking about feelings. We're talking about *blood*. Ain't that what you said? It's all of us Hoopers. We're a bad seed. I think I should be the first one you kill."

"Of course I'm not going to kill you. You're my son."

"Then it's not about blood, but about a single person that has wronged you. I remember all the time I was growing up, you told us that fighting was not a way to solve our problems. You told us to move away if we had to. Do whatever we needed to do, but not to fight.

Nathe chewed on his lower lip. He knew it was time to let the hatred go. "All right, I understand what you're saying. You're right. I'm wrong. Let's go and talk to Glee and settle this. We'll make him move. He'll pay us back for all that he's stolen, or we'll call in the law to help. Do you want to go with me?"

"I'd be glad to go with you, but you need to know something. Glee is dead."

"Dead? How? What happened? You didn't…?"

"No Papa, I didn't. He fell from Thunderhead Point. We were arguing. He swung at me and missed. He lost his footing and fell. I tried to help him, but it was more than I could do. Owen tried to help, but…"

"Owen? What was he doing up there? Was he was working for Glee helping steal my logs?"

"Yes, and that's something else we'll have to deal with in time. For now, we need to tell Glee's family what happened."

Nathe's back felt like it had a fifty-pound sack of corn on it. "We need to see if we can get the body up from out of Tucker's hell."

"I don't think that's possible. Do you? It's smack dab in the middle of Tucker's Hell, on a pile of rocks best I can figure."

"We'll likely not be able to get that body back, I don't reckon."

Nathe shook his head as he thought of where Glee lay. "The reason it's called Tucker's hell is that Papa had an uncle whose name was Tucker. Papa was his namesake. He once went into that tangled mess and never came out. At least that's what they think happened to him. His coat and gun were found lying just where you enter it from the river. His dog was not seen again either. They figured he went in to get the dog, and both got twisted up in the stand of laurel and died. It always seemed strange to me that the dog didn't come out. Even a bear can make its way out without too much trouble. Papa said a Hooper killed them both and threw them in there, if that's really where Tucker's and his dog's body ended up. Nobody knows for sure."

Nathe rolled up his sleeves and stood quietly as he looked up the mountain. Tears filled his eyes when he spoke. "I don't guess we need to go looking for the body. The buzzards will have had a field day with him by the time we got him out, even if we found him. We'd have to bury him before anybody else came around due to the smell. It'd be best to leave him there. Everybody will understand, I think."

Davie nodded. "There's a load of logs up there that are cut and loaded from their work today. What do you think we need to do about that?"

"We'll make Owen tell us where to take them to sell. We might as well get the pay. I'll give the money to Glee's wife. It's the last they'll get from a Watson. She'll, no doubt, move back in with her Papa and Mama. I hope this ends all the quarreling. Surely the rest of the Hoopers can see that taking advantage of another person brings you to a bad end. Glee got what he deserved, God rest his soul. I wouldn't want to meet my maker with what he has on his record."

Davie watched his Papa's face. "I did try to save him."

"I know. You're a finer man than I could've hoped to help raise. I'm proud of you."

Davie kicked at a rock. "He reminded me that I was a Hooper."

Nathe put his hand on Davie's shoulder. "You are, by blood, a Hooper and a Fisher, but you're a Watson to me. I knowed you wouldn't do nothing but what was right. If he could've been saved, you would've done it. I didn't mean harm talking about the Hoopers like I did just now. I know they're yore family, and you could feel hard at me for saying all that I said."

Davie squatted down. "Papa, do you think that Hooper blood in my son will someday make him mean? I know I told you that I don't believe in bad blood, but could it happen?"

"At one time, I did think that. I don't think that now. It's been too many generations of hard feelings and hatred, and all involved didn't have Hooper or Watson blood. Ever since the day I decided not to kill Glee's Papa and let bygones be bygones, I've wanted to make a difference. To stop the hateful deeds and murder. I realize there are choices a man or woman makes. Glee saw both good and bad from both the Hoopers and the Watsons, but he made up his own mind about the actions he took. You have to do the same, and that baby of yores that'll soon be here will stand before God for his own actions, as well. He won't be able to blame nobody but himself. The best you can do is to teach him the right way to live."

Davie spit on the ground between his knees. "It makes a person want to hole up in these mountains, not ever get out and rub shoulders with nobody else. Just mind yore own business and live yore own life."

"It does at that, son. But, I don't think that's possible. Not anymore. The outsiders are coming in by the droves. Schooling has its good and bad points. A man needs a fair amount of schooling, but it makes you open to new ideas, thoughts, and feelings. Things will never be the same. But, on the good side, we've pushed ourselves out away from each other, moving from one mountain to the other. One town to the next. We ain't right up in each other's face. There's less to fight about, if we ain't after the same women, land, and stock."

They both laughed.

Nathe pulled Davie to his feet. "Let's take care of business with Glee's family, and then we'll figure out what to do with Owen. Murder is not out of the question."

A smiling Nathe turned to Davie and said, "I was teasing you. But with what he's done with Glee, and all that I know is going on with Lottie, something has to be done with him. The laws don't rightly take care of a man that hits on his wife. Ain't right, but it's the truth. Don't think I could get him convicted for working for somebody else, when he could say that he didn't really know that was not Glee's land. He could have asked of course, but didn't. The law will be no help to us at all. I need to think on how to handle him. I fear if something is not done, Lottie will die at his hands before long."

Chapter 22

Lottie stood in the doorway and caught a breath of cooler air. The wind blew a steady breeze. Low rumbles of thunder rolled in the distance. She had been piecing a quilt since right after daylight when Owen left for work. She usually did quilt work at night, but, with fall coming and this baby due soon, she needed to get it done.

She was glad August had slept a little later than usual, and now she was eating a left over biscuit from breakfast that Lottie had broken open and put in a teaspoon of sugar. The two older ones had started school. The quietness of the morning let her catch her breath. This baby she carried was taking a lot out of her. She hated carrying a baby when she grew the biggest during the hot summer months, not that she had any control over when she got in the family way.

She heard yelling before she heard the hoofbeats, as they came near to her house. She stood in the door. It was Owen. The horse was in a lather from hard riding. It gasped for breath, and its sides swelled. It blew out the air and whinnied. One jump, and Owen was off the horse and standing in front of her and pushed her back into the house.

"What's wrong? What are you doin' here in the middle of the day?"

"I think you better sit down for a minute. You need to hear something from me and not someone else."

Lottie drew her dress up around her and sat down on the step. "Is it Papa? Is he dead?"

"What are you talking about? That old man is fine, I am sure. He just thinks he's dying."

"Papa is so sick. I can tell. That's why he got someone to help him make crops this summer. He never would've done that, if he hadn't been sick. He's a hard worker."

"Just shut up, and let me talk. Glee fell off the side of the mountain and was killed today."

"Killed? What was he doing so close to the side of a mountain to fall off? What are you doing up there? You never tell me nothing."

"Him and Davie was arguing, I reckon. He slid off the mountain."

Tears gathered in Lottie's eyes, and she squeezed her jaws together to keep from screaming at him. She knew he didn't like any of her family. He was going to blame Davie for this. It was of no use, she had to speak. "It couldn't have been Davie's fault."

"I never said it was Davie's fault. I was there when Glee fell. Davie was trying to save him. I tried, too. His arms and hands gave out, and he dropped."

"What were they arguing about? Davie never was a quarreler. It don't sound like him."

She looked up at Owen. He looked over her head into the house, but wouldn't look at her face. "That's the other thing I'm goin' to tell you. We've been cutting logs off yore Papa's place and some off of Davie's. Glee was selling them to the Asheville Lumber Company."

"Did Papa or Davie know? Was Papa getting a part of it?"

"No, they didn't know until now. Davie found out. That's why they were arguing. Mostly, we took the logs to Balsam by wagon and put them on the train, but sometimes the lumber company picked them up. They sent them to Asheville to be cut into boards, and they'd put them on the rail to the north for building. It's good money."

Owen went on and on about how it all happened. She didn't care a smidgen about that part. "Owen, please hush. You were stealing from my Papa. Why did you do that? I knew he was worried about something? You caused all that worry to him, just making him sicker and sicker."

"It was not me. It was Glee. I worked an honest day's work for an honest day's pay."

"Honest. You're crazier than a Bessie bug. That's not honest! You knew Papa didn't know that Glee was stealing. You knew it was not Glee's land. You're a snake in the grass. A thief."

She jumped up, held her hands under her heavy belly, and ran into the house. She slammed the door. She hated him.

"You don't slam the door in my face. Do you hear me?" He ran inside and jerked her around to face him. "I'm yore husband, and you're to defend me, not him. You left them. I feed you. I gave you these children. Everything and everyone in this house is mine. I work hard to feed you all."

"I'd rather starve than have you stealing. You've ruined our name. We'll be known as thieves all over the place. My children will be the children of a thief. I can't agree to that kind of thing, even out of my husband."

"So, am I supposed to let you starve? Or should I get any job I can to feed my family? You keep getting in the family way over and over and adding more mouths for us to feed."

"You think I did that by myself, you sorry thing? You think it wasn't yore fault too?" Lottie took August to the porch and sat her down. She pulled the woodbox over and set it on her dress tail to keep her in one place. "Play on the porch, girl. I'll come back and get you in a bit." She went back into the house.

"You get back over here to me. Don't call me names." He jerked her around again. She pulled back. "You're my wife, and you do what I say. You respect me."

"How can I respect a thief, especially one that steals from my Papa? From my own family. You don't deserve respect."

His face turned red. He put his hands on her shoulders and pushed her with all his might across the room. She slammed against the wall beside the front door.

Owen left her in the floor and rode away.

Chapter 23

Most times, Owen wouldn't let Lottie go to church, much less go with her. But the last two Sundays, he had attended. They often said the devil goes to church every time the door is open, and Lottie knew it was true for the two Sundays, for sure.

Beck reached in his pocket. He fiddled with the piece of brown paper he had used to wrap the supplies he had picked up for Nathe. He stood by a tree and watched as Sugar talked to Owen. If looks could kill, he would already be dead at the hands of Sugar. Lottie slipped between them, and Owen walked to the other side of the church yard.

Beck went to the two girls and slipped the paper he held into Lottie's hand without saying a word. He went to where his horse was tied, mounted it, and rode away.

Sugar looked from the paper to Lottie's face, then to the back of Beck as he hurried away. She looked and saw that Owen was talking to the preacher.

"What's written on there?" Sugar tried to grab the paper from Lottie.

"I don't know, but I don't think I'd better let Owen see it."

"He's clean over to the other side of the churchyard. Let me read it." Sugar tried to pull Lottie's hand from behind her back where she held the note.

Owen had walked away from the preacher. Lottie tiptoed and tried to look over people's heads to find him. When she couldn't, she walked up the hill a bit and saw him deep in conversation with two men she didn't recognize. She ran back and grabbed Sugar's hand and pulled her to a nearby tree. Lottie unfolded the paper.

Scribbled were the words, "A hole at the bottom of the cucumber tree behind yore springhouse. Letters will be there."

"What letters? Are you writing him letters?" Sugar squeaked.

Lottie folded the letter and pushed it into the top of her dress between her breasts. "This is the first note I've ever gotten from him. We don't write no letters."

"Well, he's going to be writing you one. You have to tell me what he says. When do you think he'll write?"

"I don't know. He don't say when."

Sugar put her hands on her hips and tapped her toe. "He wasn't happy with that black eye of yores. I saw the way he looked at Owen in the church. I bet he's going to get you out of this hell hole you have gotten yoreself in, or maybe he plans to kill him."

"Gotten myself in? I didn't know he was mean, or I wouldn't have married him. Surely Beck won't kill him."

"You knew all right. Our whole family knows you got the second sight. I don't' believe you weren't warned about this."

"You sound like Mama. I don't know if what I see is real or just some silly dream or thoughts I'm having. You all act like I know about all that, and I don't. It's all scary to me. It's not a good feeling to know things. I wish you had that veil over yore face instead of me. You'd know what to do with it."

"Well I didn't, and you did. You'd better get to learning how to figure these things out, or you're going to live a long, hard life."

Lottie shrugged her shoulders. "Even if you feel like you know something, there's nothing that tells you what to do about it. Like Owen. I didn't feel good about our being wed, but I figured it was all that talk from Mama and Papa about how they didn't like him. I couldn't tell the difference between what was a sign and what was the feelings that I got from them not wanting me to marry."

Sugar shook her head. "I wish it had been me that got the gift, too. Maybe then I'd have known and took you away from here. I wouldn't have let you marry him. He's evil, the devil hisself."

Lottie stared at the ground. "Spilt milk…It's too late to be crying over this. What's done is done. Nothing we can do now."

"I wouldn't count on that. I think Beck thinks he can do something. I hope he can. I'd be in favor of killing him, though." Sugar put her arm out and patted her sister on the back.

Lottie hugged Sugar. "Here comes Owen. It might be safer for everyone if you walk away before he gets here."

xxx

Five days in a row, after Owen left to look for work, Lottie went to the Cucumber tree. Yet, there was still no letter.

If he is trying to make a fool of me, he's doing a good job. Lottie looked in every direction.

"If you're out there making fun of me for looking for a letter, you've got yore laugh. Are you watching me? Laughing at me?" Lottie yelled into the wind that stirred in the Cucumber tree. "It ain't funny to me." She sat down at the bottom of the tree and put her head in her hands and cried. "It ain't funny at all. I needed you to help me. I should've known a man was not anyone to depend on. You're all alike." She spat into the air.

She put her hand down to push herself up. The dirt slid under her fingers. That was when she saw it. The paper, dirty from the soil that covered it.

Tears slid down her cheeks as she unfolded the paper. "If you're reading this, then you realize that

I couldn't put this on top of the ground as I first planned. One of the children could've found it. It could have blown away. Or worse, Owen might have seen it. I hoped you would think about that and dig around the tree."

She laughed in spite of the tears. *If he only knew I ain't half as smart as he gives me credit for.*

"I sent a letter to my family in Tennessee by a salesman that was heading that way. I should get an answer from some source in about a week. I hope you can hold out till then. Try not to make him too mad. If he hurts you again, I might just have to kill him, and we don't have time for that right now."

Lottie laughed again. *You, Beckley Radford have more in common with Sugar than you do me. You surely don't realize what you're taking on with a woman and a bunch of children to care for.*

She kept reading. "When I get an answer, and they've arranged a place for us to go, I'll let you know with another letter."

It was signed, "Beck".

Lottie folded the letter and put it between her breasts alongside the other letter that she had worn every day since she had gotten it. It was her hope written on paper. The only hope she had had for a long, long time.

xxx

There wasn't anybody else in Jackson County that wanted all three of the children Beau and Mariah were going to bring to the courts, at least not anyone they knew. Really, they didn't want anyone to have the time to make a public request.

So, when they found a judge would be in the
county, they decided to make things official.

The judge read the petition aloud, stating the
death of Dicey Mills and ending with "*The
aforesaid children, Etta, Elbert. and Essie Mills,
now in the care of Beauregard and Mariah Hoyle,
and with their mother being dead, and no other
family coming forth to assume care of them, the
Hoyles are desirous of the care, custody, and
control of said children.*

The judge looked at the family in front of him.
"Do you want to take these children into yore home
and raise them, apprentice them?"

"Yes sir, we would that they should live with
us. Not as apprentices or farmed out to us, but as
our own children."

"Then do you desire them to take yore name?"

Mariah reached out and took her husband by
the arm and nodded.

Beau looked at the children and smiled. "Yes
sir, we do want them to take the Hoyle name."

"Very well, consider these three children
yores. Do what is right by them." The judge
nodded at the man to his right, then everyone
signed the papers.

Chapter 24

Lottie made extra biscuits and put them in Owen's lunch pail along with his usual food. He left to look for a job.

She had a good feeling about today. It had been a week since the second letter, and she felt sure that Beck's family would have answered by now.

She knew she had to finish canning, but first she had to see if there was another letter. The Cucumber tree stood above the spring and shadowed it in the early morning. Earlier this spring, the tree had flowers almost like magnolias, yellowish-green in color, and sat high on the top branches of the tree. The blooms were gone, and now there was a fruit that looked like a cucumber in their place. Most of the fruit were green, but a few were ripe and were dark orange-red.

She had decided during the night, as she lay
awake hoping for good news today, that the
cucumber tree was now her favorite tree. It would
be, from the day she got the first letter until she
died.

Fruit had dropped to the ground. She stooped,
picked it up, and split it open. It showed dark red
seeds. "I wonder if they have cucumber trees in
Tennessee."

She stood up and walked around underneath
the tree, afraid to dig. She was afraid the letter
might not be there.

When she couldn't stand it any longer, she fell
on her knees and raked back the dirt where the first
letter had been. It was there! She took the letter
and pulled it to her breast, afraid to read it now that
she had it. What if his family refused to help
them? What if Beck had changed his mind? What
if he had decided he didn't want to be in the middle
of the trouble between her and Owen. Maybe he
was going to tell her that he was leaving without
her.

Once she would have daydreamed half the day
away wondering about it, saving the words to read
later. Having kids and the life she had lived made
her more practical. She sat down and opened the
letter. She read through it fast, and then laid on her
back and looked up through the trees. She pulled
her knees against her bulging belly and threw her
dress over her legs and hugged them to her. The
sun was high enough that it sent tiny streams of
light between the leaves. A light wind blew the
limbs. The movement made the light shining

through dance on the ground all around her and on the dress that covered her knees.

A smile spread across her face, and she sat up to read the letter again. This time she read it out loud. It made everything seem more real.

Lottie,

I can take you away. My family got me a job on a farm in Cosby. They said I could get extra money if I wanted to search for ginseng in the mountains. Buyers come by pretty often and buy up all that people have. They send it to China or somewhere. Said there was a lumber mill at Hartford, too. I might be able to work with them some, as I have done that kind of work before. But the farm has a house we can live in.

Lottie looked at the writing. He wrote good. Nice even letters. No smudges. He seemed really smart.

You need to bring a bag with a change of clothes for you and each child, and hide it at the end of the road that goes to yore Papa's house. We'll meet there Thursday after Owen goes to look for work. That'll give us a head start. I don't have a wagon, but I'll try to borrow one. We'll take that up to Waynesville and get on a train that will take us to a town in Tennessee. A friend will meet us there. Don't tell nary a soul that we're leaving. Somebody might tell, and they could be in real danger, if Owen finds out they know.

If you don't show up, I'll know you've changed yore mind.

                    Beck

She folded the letter neatly and slipped it into her bosom with the others.

XXX

Beck knocked on the frame around the door at Nathe's. The door stood open, and he could see both Nathe and Addie sitting at the table, a pot of coffee sitting on a block of wood between then.

"Come on in Beck. What are you doing here today? I told you we could take today off. That last field of corn is not ready for the pulling yet."

Beck coughed and scrubbed the bottom of his shoe against the wooden porch floor. "Could I talk to you outside for a bit?"

Nathe looked at Addie then back at Beck and nodded. "I'll be right out. Just meet me out by the barn."

The horse nickered as Beck led him to the barn and tied him to a pole by the walnut tree. When he turned around, Nathe had left the porch and was halfway between him and the house. Beck walked to meet him.

"I know there are a couple more weeks of work here, but I was wondering if I could get what money is coming to me. It's about time I move on. Got some things I need to do that's a good piece from here, and I don't think I'll be coming back for some time."

Nathe took off his hat and raked his hand through his thinning grey hair. "I really hadn't expected you to leave yet."

"And I hadn't planned to, sir, but something has come up. It's really important, or I wouldn't ask."

Nathe reached out and patted him on the shoulder. "I believe that. You've been nothing but honest and hardworking and, if you say it's important, I believe you. Let me think for a moment."

Beck swallowed so hard he made a gulping sound. Nathe looked at him and then back toward the house. "You stay here. I have to run something by Addie. I'll be right back."

Beck nodded. He twisted his hat in circles with his hands. He was having second thoughts about what he was doing. *What if he don't let me have that money? I can't get me, Lottie, and the children out unless he does. I may have got her hopes up for nothing. Worse than that, I might get her killed, if she attempts to leave before I could let her know that we'd have to wait. I don't have another plan if this doesn't happen.*

A rush of breath in relief came through Beck's lips as he saw Nathe counting money as he walked back toward the barn.

Beck reached to get the money, but Nathe pulled it out of his reach.

"I thought…" Beck began.

"It's fine. I'll give you the money, but I have a few things to say to you first."

"Sure. I understand." Beck said with relief.

"Come on with me to the barn. I need you to listen to me good." They walked, and Nathe continued to talk. "I have a gut feeling that this involves Lottie somehow."

Beck bit his lip, and didn't say yay or nay.

"I really don't know whether to say thank you or beat you half to death. There's not a doubt in my or Addie's mind that, if Lottie stays here, at

some point, she's going to be found dead at the
hand of that good-for-nothing husband of hers.
There are good reasons for her leaving, that I know
to be true. But there's the fact that I don't know
you as well as I should. Are you going to be good
to her? And we're not sure we'll ever see her
again."

Tears filled Nathe's eyes. Beck looked toward
the house. Addie stood in the door with one hand
over her heart and holding a cloth to her nose with
the other.

Nathe continued. "I don't want you to say a
word. It'll be best for my family if I can honestly
say I have no idea where you are or where Lottie
is. The one thing I'm going to tell you is that
you'd better take care of her. Take care of those
children like they were yore own, just like I did
Davie when I married Addie. Even though he was
not my own flesh and blood, I don't think anyone
can say I've treated him any different than those
that is my own flesh and blood.'"

When Beck started to speak, Nathe raised his
hands. "Not one word. Keep listening. There is a
wagon for sale over on Dark Ridge. I put a little
extra money with yore pay. Go buy that wagon.
You'll have those youngins to think about, and a
wagon will be needed. Don't tell nobody I did
that. Addie don't even know about that. There's
enough money there to buy her a horse when you
get to where you're going. I want her to have one."

Beck nodded.

"Another thing, you assure Lottie that, no
matter what happens, we all love her. There's

nothing we wouldn't do for her if we could. The mainst thing we can do now is to let her go. Someday, I hope we can see her and the children again. Until then, I'm depending on you to do what is right by her. When you can, and if you love her, you marry her and make this honest. Hopefully, that won't be long."

When he realized that Nathe didn't plan on saying anything else, Beck reached out and laid his palm up. Nathe laid the money in his hand. Beck reached out and grabbed Nathe and hugged him tight. He waved goodbye to Addie that still stood in the doorway. He went to his horse and rode away.

xxx

Owen left long before daylight. He had gotten a job with a crew building bridges for the railroad. Lottie took a pillow case off her pillow and pushed clothes into it. Then, she took the case off Owen's pillow and packed it with the children's clothes. The only other thing that she took from the house was the picture of her family they'd made at the church. Papa had made sure each one of the children got one. They had delivered them the week before. It was all she might have to remember them by.

She woke the children and dressed them. Light peeked over the mountain when she shoved them out the door. It was enough light to barely see the path they needed to take.

When she got to the end of the road at her Papa's, Beck hadn't shown up. She knew she shouldn't, but she hid the pillow cases in the weeds and took the kids up to the house.

Sugar sat on the back step chewing a black gum twig and rubbing it against her teeth. "What are you doing here this early? The children are with you, too. Is this something we were talking about the other day?"

"Can't say right now." Lottie looked at the children standing in a row by her side.

Sugar stood up and grabbed Annie May by the hand. "You children get in the house. Yore grandma has jelly and biscuit. Bet you're hungry."

They looked at Lottie, begging with their eyes.

"Get on in there and eat. We've to get back down the road in a few minutes."

When they were inside, Lottie sat down by Sugar. "He sent a letter to meet him down the road this morning, but I was not to tell nobody. You can't tell a soul, Sugar. I could be putting you in harm's way just for knowing this. Owen would kill you to find out where I am."

"Well, if he kills me, he won't ever find out. So I guess he'll just be bluffing, if he threatens to do that. Besides, I don't rightly know what house you're going to. I don't know what part of the country. But if it's where Beck lived before, it'll be easy for Owen to find that out."

"It's not in that town. It's a little ways from there, but he has kin nearby. Just not real close family. He'll have a job and everything. We have a house to move into where we can live."

"Looks like Beck planned this out real good. Sounds like he might've been planning this awhile."

Lottie frowned. "I don't think so. It was just after seeing my black eyes at the funeral it all started. He don't seem to want anything from me, just to make it safe for me and the children." She watched Sugar's face and realized she didn't agree. "You don't believe that, do you?"

Sugar's chest rose. She took a deep breath and waited to give her answer to Lottie. "I don't trust men much anymore. What with Owen being like he is, and with the likes of Tolliver Chastain." Tears filled her eyes.

"What did Tolliver do? I thought he asked you to marry him."

"He did. Even went and got a marriage license. I thought he meant he wanted to marry me. That sounds like it to you, don't it? Getting a marriage license? Anybody would've thought that, right? I'm not crazy, am I?"

Lottie put her arm around Sugar's shoulders. "It sounds that way to me. I would've thought that was what he planned. What happened?"

After a bit, Sugar looked at Lottie. Her lips pushed together and stuck them out. Her face turned red, and she started to cry, really hard. She shook like a leaf in the wind, shivering like she was in the midst of a winter chill. "He took advantage of me. Told me we were going to marry next week anyway. Then after he took advantage of me, he tore that paper up into a thousand pieces, and threw it in the wind. He laughed and laughed at me while I cried. He said, 'You think I'd want to marry the likes of you? You're just trash. Yore family has bad blood. They fight and kill and have since they come to this country my Papa said.' I started retching and gagging, and he just laughed more."

Lottie pulled Sugar into her arms and hugged her tightly. "Oh baby girl, I'm so sorry. He's just one of those sorry men that lie to get what they want. All men are not like that. Owen is, and it seems Tolliver is, too. But there are good ones. There's Papa, and Beck seems really good. Don't let that Chastain boy know he hurt you. He's not good enough for you to wipe yore feet on. He's the one that's trash."

Sugar raised her head and stared into the distance. "I did love him, you know. He was good to me for a long time. Don't you let Beck treat you like you let Owen. Men can act good sometimes, and then get mean." Sugar looked straight into Lottie eyes. "Promise me you won't let him hurt you like you let Owen. If you don't promise me that, I'll kill them both today. I'll get Papa's gun and hunt them both down."

"I promise. I promise. It's taken a lot of courage for me to leave. You know that, right?"

Sugar nodded.

"I've gone too far to change now. Being beat up on won't happen to me again. Whatever it takes, I'll not live with another man that's mean to me again. I'll die first, die making him sorry he tried to hurt me."

Addie came out on the porch. She wiped her hands on her apron. "I fed the young'uns. I don't rightly know where you're going and not sure I want to."

Lottie held up her hand. "Mama, I have something to ask you. With the way you know things, did you know what Glee was doing and what Owen was helping him with?"

"I did, and you are going to ask me why I didn't tell anyone. Nathe wanted me to tell him what they were doing from the first, and I wouldn't. Actually, I couldn't. I knew if he could coax me to tell him, Nathe would kill Glee. I was hoping it would all straighten itself out on its own. I hoped that Glee would leave the county before there was bloodshed. I decided it was best to not tell yore Papa. He needed to eat this hog one bite at a time. That way he could swallow between bites and let his anger subside somewhat. Some things are better learned in small slices of time instead of all at once."

"I just needed to know." There were tears in Lottie's eyes.

"You'll learn what to tell, and what not to." Addie went to the water bucket and washed her hands. "Back to what's going on today. And before you ask, no I don't know. For some reason, I had no warning. I know Beck quit working for us last night, and he said he had business out of town. Yore Papa suspected he was taking you with him. Now, you show up telling us you're leaving. I figure yore Papa is right, and the two are tied together somehow. At first I wanted to turn you over my knee and give you the whupping of yore life, but yore Papa said it's the only thing left to keep you alive. I think he might be right. I have to hear from you sometime. I just need to know you're alive." She started to cry.

"Mama, don't cry, or I'll cry too. The children don't need to see me crying right now. I ain't told them much about where we're going or why. So far, they ain't asked a lot of questions...being satisfied that we're going visiting. Beck will take care of me. I'm sure of it. Someday we'll be back together."

"There's a voice in my ear saying that ain't so, baby girl. But knowing you're alive will make it worth being apart. Just promise you'll let me know you're alive and how my grandchildren are."

There was a sound of a horse in full gallop coming up the road. Lottie knew it couldn't be Beck, because he'd said he would get a wagon for them. Lottie ran in the house to hide. She peeked out the window.

"I have a telegram for Nathe and Addie Watson."

"I'm Addie." Addie was pale as a ghost.

The rider handed her the paper and left.

Lottie ran back outside. Nobody said a word. They looked at each other and back to the paper in Addie's hand. Finally, Addie said, "I heard tell about these, but I ain't never seen one before. I guess we ought to read it."

Sugar took it from her mother's shaking hands and unfolded it. She glanced over the words, and then back to her Mama. "Maggie, get Mama a chair and have her sit down. Get Lottie one too. Lottie, come and sit by Mama."

There were tears in Sugar's eyes as she sat down at the feet of her mother and read, "Asa killed (stop) Particulars sent with body on train arriving today at two o'clock (stop) Our condolences (stop)."

Addie leaned over and took the paper from Sugar. She pulled it to her heart and screamed. "My boy. My sweet boy is gone."

Sugar shouted out orders like a general in the army. "Maggie, get out to the tobacco field, and get Papa. Don't tell him what's happened until he gets here. Just say Mama needs him, then hightail it on back here. He'll follow you."

Sugar showed that day what Lottie had always known about her. She may have been the baby, but she was the strongest one in the bunch. She hurt like the rest of them, but she knew what had to be done and did it. She could hold things inside for a long time, maybe forever.

Lottie and Sugar helped Mama inside. She made them stop at the clock. She reached inside and stopped the pendulum from swinging. They took her to the bed where she quarled up like a baby with her face to the wall and cried. Her quaking body shook the bed.

Lottie pulled Sugar to the side. "She's afraid if she don't stop that clock, somebody else will die. She's worried about Papa."

"I know. If she hadn't stopped the clock, I would've." Sugar looked at Lottie. "But Papa was not who I was worried about being the second to die if we didn't stop the clock. You know who was in my thoughts."

Lottie nodded her head. "What do I do? I can't leave here now. Mama and the rest of you need me."

Sugar stared at Lottie and seemed in deep thought. "You have to go now. It's yore only chance. We'll be with Mama and Papa. There's nothing you can do. Git yoreself and those children to where it's safe."

At Lottie's sad face, Sugar continued, "I know you want to be here with Asa when his body comes back. But I figure, if he was hurt on his job, and because it's been a few days, we can't rightly lay him out for all to see. So, you won't be able to see him no how."

Lottie cried when Sugar pushed her to the door and said, "Git those kids out of here. Git on down the road to meet Beck before the word gets to Owen. He'll come here thinking you're probably here with us. As for later, if you send letters, you'd better find a secret way to do it. Owen's family is close knit to others in town, especially those at the post office, and he'll hear you wrote. But do find a way to let us know how you're doing. Mama will need it, even more now than she would have before. You don't have to worry about Mama and Papa. I'll take care of them as long as I need to. I don't plan on ever marrying no how, after all I've been through."

Lottie grabbed Sugar and hugged her tight. "I love you, baby sister. It's not right leaving you here like this."

"I've got Maggie to help. The others will come as they can. Don't worry none about us. Make a new life, and keep yoreself safe." Sugar pulled herself out of Lottie's grip and pushed her to the edge of the steps. "Now git on down the road to Beck. Now."

xxx

Lottie kept telling the kids to move a little faster. She could see the wagon ahead and Beck was sitting in it. She was glad he hadn't left.

"Beck, Beck. I'm so sorry we're late."

"I knew you were here. I saw the two sacks of clothes in the bushes. Hope you didn't tell anyone where we're going."

"No. You told me not to, and I didn't. You're right. It wouldn't be safe for them to know, especially now."

Beck jumped down from the wagon. "Why now? Did something happen? Does Owen know you're gone?"

"No, nothing like that. But a horseman came today with a telegram for Mama and Papa. Asa got killed near Asheville where he was working."

Beck reached out and put his hand on her shoulder. Lottie looked up and bit her lower lip, trying not to cry.

"Oh Lottie, I'm sorry. You probably don't want to go with me now, but I don't know if we can plan it for another time. I quit work from yore Papa and sent word we're on our way. What are we going to do?"

Lottie made a fist and used her knuckles to wipe away the tears that ran down the sides of her nose. "I'm going with you now. I didn't git to say a proper goodbye to Mama because she'd taken to the bed in her sorrow, and Papa had not come in from the field yet. But Sugar will tell them. She made me come. She's knows I'm leaving, just not where I'm going. But, if Owen hears about Asa, he'll come looking for me at Papa's house, thinking I'll be there. It gives us less time. He won't go by our house and find me missing first like I'd hoped."

Beck helped the children into the back of the wagon and threw the clothes beside them. He reached for Lottie's hand. "Let me help you. Be careful with yore belly. When is this baby due to be born anyway?"

Lottie sat down and put her hands on her stomach. "About any day now. My back has been hurting all morning. Hope it's not today. We'd better get on down the road."

Beck drove as quickly as he could, trying not to hit the bumps in the road for fear of putting Lottie into birth pangs.

"Mama, are we ever coming back here?" Brody stood on his knees and placed his hand on Lottie's shoulder. "Why is Papa not going with us? Will we ever see him again?"

Beck and Lottie looked at each other. "We have to go away for a little while. You may see him someday again, but not for a while. You have to be a big boy and help me with the other children. I need you not to cry about this."

Brody made a face. "Ain't planning on crying. I know more than you think I do. I'm glad we're going away."

Annie May sniffed. "I ain't glad. What will Papa do without us?"

Beck spoke without looking back at her. "He'll do just fine. He'll work and go right on living."

Annie May stuck her lower lip out in a pout. "He might not do good. He won't have Mama to cook or raise a garden or can the food. Who'll wash his clothes?"

Only loud enough for Lottie to hear Beck said, "Who will he beat on, with all you being gone?"

"Shhhh. Don't say that." Lottie folded her hands in her lap and squeezed them hard.

Annie May reached up and hit Brody's arm with her fist. "Don't you love Papa?"

"You're just a baby, you don't understand nothing." Brody pushed her hand away.

Beck was tired of the fussing. "That's enough. Just sit down and hush. We'll be at the train in a little while."

"A train?" All three said together.

xxx

Owen waited in the barn until Nathe brought the horse inside to put it in the stable. Nathe slid the latch on the stable into place and patted the horse on the neck. "I'll get a block of hay for you, old boy."

When he turned away from the door, an arm went across his shoulder and, in one swoop he was pinned against the wall.

"Where's my wife?"

"I don't know but, if I did, I wouldn't tell you. She's a smart woman to leave the likes of you."

"You better tell me where she is. If you don't, and if I have to find her on my own, I'll kill her. There ain't no woman gonna make a fool of me."

Nathe laughed in his face. "I'd say you don't need any help doing that. You do a pretty good job all by yoreself. Yore quick temper has made you a fool. Everybody knows it."

He pulled Nathe to him, and then slammed him hard against the wall. "You better not cross me. Tell me where she is now, or else."

"I'm not afraid of you. You may have made my Lottie afraid, but you shore don't scare me. You should be glad she left, for if she'd stayed, you'd be dead. You'd be lying up in those mountains until yore body rotted."

Owen pulled his leg up and put his knee into Nathe's stomach. He reached down and pulled out a knife and put it to Nathe's throat.

The knife flew across the barn, hit a board, and flipped into a stable. Owen hit the dirt, and dust and hay seed went into the air. "Don't lay a finger on my Papa again, or this is nothing compared to what will happen to you next time." Cling rubbed his hand on his leg trying to ease the pain in his fist.

"Git out of here, and don't come back to this house again. None of us know where Lottie is but, if we did, there's not a soul here that hadn't rather die than tell you. There may be people in town that like yore family and will stand up for you, but out here you're nothing. And, as you've said before, loud and clear, Hoopers and Watson make their own set of rules. Rule one is that Owen Thompson is an egg-sucking dog and good for nothing, not worthy of the air he sucks in during the day or night. So we don't want to see you again."

Owen got up and took one step toward Cling but stopped when Beau came in and stood by Cling. Owen grabbed his hat and run out.

"Don't think we'll be seeing any more of him. But if he comes around, just let me know." Cling took his Papa's arm, and they went to the house.

Chapter 25

The first letter from Lottie came by the same friend that Beck had used to carry letters to his family. The man peddled items to the mountains brought in by train from the North, farming equipment and the like.

Maggie and Sugar got it first and read it.

Dear Mama and Papa and rest of family,

I sure do miss y'all. I wonder how you all are, and if Papa is doing okay. I still can't tell you where we are. This here peddler that brought the letter to you goes a little of everywhere. That keeps our whereabouts secret enough. I guess I can tell you the name of the road we live on. It's called Booger Holler. It's plum scary up here in this dark valley. I keep expectin' a booger to come out any time I'm out at night. Mama, you know I always was a fraidy-cat.

We got a house to live in. It ain't much, but it's a roof over our head in bad weather. So, I'm thankful for it. Beck thinks he might get a different job at a Tannery that just started up. If so, he'll look for a house a little nearer where he'll work. Not that beggars can be choosers, but I hope it's a little bigger than this one and not quite so drafty. Winter is coming on and I think this house may be too cold on the babies. Speaking of babies, you have a new grandchild. My baby was a boy. I named him Western Sheffield, because we rode the Western Carolina Railroad. We call him Sheffield. Can you believe me and the children rode the railroad? Sheffield was born the day after we got here, and Beck's family got me a granny woman to help.

Got lots of work to do, so need to stop and get to the peddler to bring this here letter to you. Beck said he could arrange for him to pick up a letter from you. He knows not to tell anyone where we are, but that way I can hear from you. Please write me. I miss you awful bad.

Lottie and children

Ann Robbins Phillips

Dear Daughter,

I am writing this letter as your Mama is with Mariah. She was going to have another baby, but she lost it yesterday. That was the fourth one she has lost. I am so thankful that she adopted the others so she will have someone to take care of her when she is old. The more babies she loses, the harder it is on her it seems. She cries for days and days.

Sugar is taking good care of us. She says she will never marry. She's the usual sweet girl, Sugar, until you mention men to her. She hates them and the ground they walk on. If her word holds true, she'll never marry. I wish she would change her mind. She says her lot in life is to tend to her Papa and Mama. I told her she could do that and marry, but she just laughs at me. The only time I see her cry is when your letters come or we mention you, which is nearly every day or two.

Got to meet the peddler at the end of the road at noon, so better close now. Write soon. We love you, daughter.

Papa

Dear Mama and Papa:

Papa, I am so glad you are doing better. You see, I knew you would not die like the doctor said. We need you too bad.

I miss you so badly. I would like to come home and see you. Beck said if I came back, even for a visit, that Owen would probably kill me. Maybe even you and Mama. He knows where we are. Well, at least where we used to live. He told lies to some people, saying that Beck stole his horse. The people fired him on the spot. We are now in Cocke County Tennessee, and Beck has got himself a job at a Tannery in Newport. He says it smells just awful in there, but at least it's a job.

If anything ever happens to Owen, and he dies for some reason, will you all let me know so I can come back to visit. Send a letter about how he died. Mama, I keep seeing Owen in a hole in the ground. If my second sight is real like you say, this may be a sign. His eyes are set in his head, and they're all cloudy. He's not in no casket, and there is dirt on every part of him but his face. Promise me you will write if he dies.

I have to quit writing now and get this to the peddler to bring to you. I love you both. Tell Cling, Mariah, Maggie, and Sugar that I said I love them. Tell Sugar that not all men are bad. There are a few good ones. Beck is good to us. Papa was always good to us. She is not to measure everyone's corn by Owen's half bushel.

Your loving daughter,   Lottie.

Epilogue

It's sad to me that families move apart from each other, but I guess it may be the lesser of two evils, as it is with Lottie. It's easier to know she is doing good, even if it's only known by her letters, than to think that she is being mistreated.

Sadder to me is the fact that lives come and go in this world. Time is an enemy and moves on without us, almost as if we were never here. Our influence is gone from the family. That can be either good or bad. I realize that Lottie and her family will go through life with no knowledge of me, except for stories Nathe told them, but they will forget to tell them to their children. My hope had been in a few strong words of guidance to Nathe during his life. There was no way to do it, but in the ghostly manner I used. I am trapped in the past, one that Nathe does not remember, and I cannot make him understand. In my death, I found truth and wisdom I needed to pass on, beliefs and values to teach. Hopefully, I planted seeds in Nathe that found their way into his children. There will be many generations to come. How long do such truths linger in the hearts of families? It lasts until someone fails to pass it to their children and grandchildren. If one generation fails to tell them, evil will live again, whether it be a Hooper, Watson, or any other name.

Lottie and her family have much sorrow to endure in the days to come. I will not be there to guide them. There will be many miles between Nathe and his beloved daughter, Lottie, but his influence will be in the things he taught her when she was near to him in both body and heart.

I have enjoyed my visit to my grandson. Little had changed since when I was here. But things are going to change much too fast now. It's time to say good-bye. I leave you with this advice, be you friend or foe. Find the oldest living relative you can find. Listen to their stories and the wisdom they have acquired. Find a way to weave it into the life you now live. There are some values that should never change, some truths that do not need to be altered to fit your life today. Don't let that family member pass into eternity without putting down their stories for those that are still to come, long after you are also gone.

X Amps

The End

Check out the *beginning* of this four book series by
reading
REVENGE
By Ann Robbins Phillips

Coming Fall of 2013
Read more about Lottie, Beck, and their family in
The third book in this series,
"Sorrow"

Made in the USA
Charleston, SC
11 February 2013